This is a work of fiction. Names, charac
either are products of the author's in
fictitiously. Any resemblance to actual events or locales or
persons, living or dead, is entirely coincidental.

By the same Author

Themis Series Book Two: Tell Me There's a Reason
Themis Series Book Three: Just a Badge
Available on Amazon

We Were Swans

GJ Freeman

"All humankind is born of the same inner goodness and fundamental ruthlessness as all the other creatures of nature. Man can never totally divorce himself from the beast that comprises part of his essential nature. It is not that our inner natures are entirely self-centred or completely filled with goodness. We can choose to make moral or immoral choices."

Dead Toad Scrolls

Kilroy J. Oldster

Contents

The 5th Horseman 4

Guilt 5

A Way out 23

Christian 33

Changeling 56

The Hole 64

The Darkweb 82

Sacha 94

The Jedi 143

Boot Camp 180

The Twins 212

Devon 217

Ropework 250

Epilogue 272

The 5th Horseman

The Four Horsemen had a brother. An implacable, remorseless sibling, wielding a ferocious blade that cut deep, slicing my soul and hacking chunks of wet flesh from me, digging, rooting out my core. Blood ran its length from the cross guard to the point, then sprayed, arcing, reflecting in white hot eyes that glared pitilessly in accusation. He rode me relentlessly, day in, day out. Intolerably heavy, my muscles creaked beneath him, groaning, rotting threatening to split like an ancient shipwreck. Physically broken, sunk, I waited, praying for my mind to snap, but there was no rest for me, not even in my dreams, especially not in my dreams. When too weary to hold them open, when I dared to shut my eyes, instead of sleep, my eyelids became a simple, black screen where projections of my worst nightmares flickered interminably from then to now and back again.

No, there was no peace to be found in this life, not for me. I was tired and I was drunk. Red rimmed eyes looked out from my face, staring at the bottle that was lending me courage, then at my hoard, the pills that I knew would get him off my back, release me…

Guilt

February 12th 2012

An intense police search for missing toddler, Ellen Hood, has resulted in the discovery of the body of a child. The three-year-old was reported missing during a shopping trip by her distraught Mother, Sacha. Police are appealing for witnesses and have taken away security camera footage from The Markham Shopping Centre for study. Police are attempting to contact Ellen's Father, Tom Hood, currently abroad on business and apparently unaware of his only child's disappearance.

Tom and Sacha Hood would never have claimed to be a happy family. Not that they weren't, they simply never felt the need to quantify their contentment. And if the need to calculate it had ever arisen, they would probably have done no more than show you their daughter, Ellen. The child had arrived at the right time in Tom's life. Mature enough for the responsibility but young enough for when the time came, to endure the rough and tumble of playtime with a growing youngster. At 28, he had married Sacha, 4 years his junior. Sacha, one of life's enthusiasts, auburn hair, honest blue eyes and the widest, most generous smile Tom had ever had aimed at him. They'd met online, on a dating website. In Victoria's era, courtship might have involved a carriage and a chaperone. The latter part of the twentieth century saw it evolve into pubs, nightclubs, the workplace, even the occasional supermarket encounter. Now, partnerships could be hatched electronically. It was the new way.

They both knew they had something straight off the bat. They bounced off each other. Intelligent and articulate, her typed responses matched Tom's sense of fun going from the whimsical to the bizarre and back again turning a messaging session into something more than a simple hunt for a mate.

They progressed to allowing access to their social media accounts and on her pages, a potted history illustrated someone normal. Not thousands of 'friends' harvested worldwide to fulfil any need for acceptance or sense of self-worth, just a small group going back to schooldays in the U.S. and forward to the present, here in England. Book and music 'likes' reflected her femininity and interest in the world around her. Nothing wacky or overtly political. No campaigns, no vitriol, no raging against the machine. Simply an individual with a life. But it was the photographs that bewitched him.

Scrolling through her Facebook account showed that over the years fashion had influenced her hairstyles and while not slavishly following the trend of the day, there was the occasional eccentricity in evidence. Rebelling in her teens, he guessed. Conventionally appealing, she had good bones and skin tone but there was something else about her face, her expression, that caught his attention. Attractive for sure, but there was an evident candour, an openness of expression and a light in her eyes. A zest for life that beguiled him. His own page; a bit of family, Rugby, and Supertramp. Though basic and certainly lightweight in comparison, its lack of depth clearly didn't deter her interest in him.

They exchanged phone numbers and on hearing her voice for the first time, husky, transatlantic, confirmed that she was indeed, American, born in Great Falls, Montana. Her mother had died young and her father, having recently gone the same way, had been USAF resulting in tours abroad, one of which had been in the UK. She'd liked the lifestyle here so much and having little in the way of family in the States, had opted to make England her home, moving here permanently a few years back.

Their first conversations had been tentative but over the weeks, these grew into long exchanges where they'd talk about nothing and everything and quietly hope they were both real. A few weeks later, they met. She'd phoned from a friend's wedding. She was the only single girl there and needed a man. Would Tom come? It was typically impetuous.

Friends without having laid eyes on each other and they both knew they were taking a chance, but if not now, then when? Tom drove the hundred miles or so arriving just in time for the evening reception. Meeting outside the hotel, he'd tripped on the kerb as they'd walked towards each other. It couldn't have started sweeter, his denials that he'd fallen for her met with a low, throaty chuckle. It may not have been love at first sight but for sure they felt there was something going on that neither of them ever wanted to stop.

Twelve months later, after some domestic, mental, and social adjustment, Ellen was born. Tom worked for an airline and travelled a good deal. Sacha was HR in a multi-national. Good jobs, good people, leading the good life, living the dream. In the centre of their world, Ellen.

As the engines grumbled to a full stop, he felt the soft thump of the airbridge engaging and moments later, heard the forward door crack open. A stewardess loomed, beckoning, his carry on in her hand. His status within the airline meant he invariably travelled Club Class, which always boarded and deplaned ahead of other passengers but mid-flight, the cabin crew had sought him out and though unable to explain why, told him he'd be met by police on arrival and VIP'd off.

Despite his familiarity with it, jet lag was an occupational hazard and one he'd never quite overcome. Brain fogged and dull eyed, though acknowledging the words, not all of them registered immediately. Then, slowly, the foreign word surfaced, bobbing into his consciousness.

He was used to mid-flight intrusions. Operational issues that couldn't wait but a Police presence? This was new.

The old familiarity and anticipation at being home was now edged with an anxiety he couldn't shake off. He made the airbridge threshold and was immediately hustled to a side exit, down the steel stairway and onto the ramp. Unburnt avgas, the crackle of a cooling aircraft, a fuel truck, caterers, the usual gathering of personnel who had to be there. A sense of normalcy usurped by downcast eyes and flanked by his Station Manager, a stranger; suited, official looking and clearly troubled. His policeman, he guessed, his guts churning.

There was no good news to be found in that face or, glancing around, in any face close at hand. Tom saw tears in most eyes and without knowing why but suddenly fearful, fought to control his own. Alan Jameson, head of operations in New York, had sought him out and handed him a ticket, 'You're needed back home.'

No explanation, just a ride out. Now he had a distressed policeman and colleagues he'd known for years apparently unable to look him in the eye. These were people trained to cope and in their devastated expressions, something told him that life as he had known it these past 3 years, was over.

"Where is my wife?" They were the only words he could muster, the only normal utterance he could contrive.

"At the hospital." Said the suited man, stepping forward and gently but firmly taking Tom by the elbow.

A mean flicker of hope passed through him. *At least Sacha was still....*

The spokesman noted the light of optimism in Tom's eyes and could think of nothing crueller than allowing it to burn.

"I'm sorry, Mr. Hood. It's better we talk in the car."

Confused by Sacha's stated presence at the hospital and the morgue like atmosphere of the airbridge, Tom allowed himself to be led away. A dark Range Rover waited where normally a baggage truck might be.

"Unmarked. The press is all over the place."

"But what about...?" Tom stammered, desperate for the normalcy of Customs and Immigration. He fished in his jacket pocket and pulled out a dog-eared passport.

"Taken care of." The policeman put his hand over the document. "One of my men will clear your bags."

The rear door was opened for him, and Tom slumped inside. Other doors opened and closed, and Tom became aware the vehicle was moving. "My wife? At the hospital?"

The policeman had to end it. Now. Knowing that this wasn't the kind of conversation he could go into blind, he'd spoken to some of Tom's colleagues while waiting for the aircraft to touch down. They'd told him Tom was a direct, straight to the point kind of guy so that's how he was going to handle this.

"My name is Detective Inspector Stuart Ames. I wish I had better news for you but unfortunately, there really isn't any other way to say this." He paused, then continued, reluctantly, in police speak.

"The body of a three-year-old girl has been found. This is a murder investigation. Your wife has gone to the hospital to formally establish the child's identity."

"My wife? Not in the hospital but at it?"

The difference in status was huge and his relief immediate but short lived, as Tom suddenly recognised the reference to a child, a murdered child. The enormity of it struck home at the same time as the logic. "Are there any other three-year old's missing?"

"To the best of my knowledge, Mr. Hood, no." Ames paused briefly as if the next sentence finalised the affair as, in truth, it often does. "I'm so very sorry." Ames waited.

"Are we going to the hospital now?" Tom asked softly. He wasn't looking anywhere, not seeing anything. Eyes down, just listening.

"To the Station." Ames paused. "It's more secure than the hospital. I've asked my officers to bring your wife there as soon as she's ready. You'll have some privacy there and of course, there are formalities we must go through. It can't be helped. After that, well, that's up to you but I don't think either of you should go home, at least not for the time being. We'll both know more when we get to the station."

As a reflex, Tom covered his eyes. They were red, gritty, and sore from lack of sleep. Going east to the States was easy but coming back west to east, the jet lag was a killer unless you slept your way home as Tom usually tried to do. There had been no chance of that this time. The nature of his departure had played on his mind but with no information to go on he'd tried to push speculation aside.

He concentrated hard on his work, took his job seriously and did it well. He could think of no operational Doomsday scenario he wasn't prepared for and had tried to relax, confident that whatever the emergency in the U.K. was, he had it covered. That the sudden return home might be related to his family hadn't even crossed his mind.

Thoughts of work unravelled, faded, disappeared. Stopped mattering. Though an emotional man, he had always tried to hide his feelings, suffering in silence rather than giving vent to overt displays.

"Oh, God." The whispered, unconscious, and unanswered plea escaped his lips. At that moment, there was nothing left to say and only one possible thing to do. He thought of Ellen. His golden child, his world. His eyes brimmed with tears and his throat constricted, shoulders shaking, Tom bowed his head and let go. Sobbing quietly, for the first time since Ellen had been born, Tom cried. Full realisation would come later but meanwhile, Tom just cried. The girl was dead. The girl was dead. *Cope dammit.*

Inside the station more shocked faces had greeted him as he'd been led to a small waiting room. Ames left, saying he'd be back shortly. For the moment, and having nothing else to do, Tom sat and waited, thinking about the journey here. *What has happened? How did it happen?*

Ames had understated the presence of the press. They weren't just all over the place. They were everywhere. As they'd exited the airport ramp through the fenced gate. An attempted pursuit down the motorway. As they'd entered the police compound. It was madness, cameras had even taken up vantage points to overlook the station's car park. Ames had been right. They wouldn't be able to go home, as if that mattered. Then a thought struck him, something that did matter.

Candidly, as if separated from reality, a notion that young children become victims every day went through his mind. What was it that made his daughter so special? Distracted, he checked his phone. Nothing. Then he remembered, it was still in aircraft mode. An unconscious decision left it that way. The door opened and Ames came into the room.

"Will you tell me what happened? Why all this? Has Sacha arrived yet?"

Ames sat opposite and placed two cups of tea on the small table. "I carry a hip flask if you'd like a drop in your tea?"

It was easier for Tom to nod than to shake his head. It seemed to him also that Ames needed time to prepare, to present, to tell him what had happened to his child.

"My people at the hospital have been in touch. Your wife won't be meeting us here. She's been sedated. It would be best if she stayed that way at least for tonight. The body, you see…"

Tom looked up from his tea. The policeman appeared to be late thirties, perhaps early forties. He wore a smart suit which was sharply in contrast to his rumpled, careworn expression. What was most apparent to Tom though, were his eyes. They looked tired and were trying not to say too much.

"Mr. Ames," he said softly, "sooner or later the full details will come out. I'd rather have them straight from the horse's mouth, so to speak, avoid unnecessary distress, that sort of thing. Then. If it's ok with you, I'd like to be with my wife. Given what you've said, what's happened, surely anything else can wait until tomorrow. I think I need to be with her."

Ames was not your average policeman. A University graduate, his first career had been as a lawyer. He'd practised for a time until a belief developed that the distance between the law and justice was too wide for his conscience to straddle. In his latter career as a policeman, understanding the first had better enabled him to deliver the second, and he'd seen every species of criminal; every outrage man was capable of perpetrating. Or thought he had.

Part of his mind dealt with what he had to say, another, with how he'd say it. The man in front of him was wounded and was about to suffer further damage. There was an inevitability to that, he had to be told. There was never a right time but, in the moment, he estimated that Hood was detached, focussing on the peripheral while absorbing events. This kind of split clarity was not unusual, but it wouldn't last. While it did, he'd relate the facts and let the unavoidable questions take care of the less palatable aspects of the crime.

"We already have the killers."

"Plural?"

"There were two of them. Your wife was out shopping. In one of the bigger clothing stores, they were briefly separated by aisles of hanging racks. As soon as your wife realised she couldn't see Ellen, she called out for her, hearing nothing and still unable to see her, she went looking. It really was only a matter of seconds, but unfortunately, she'd gone. Simply disappeared."

"She's a sod for it." Said Tom, still partially disconnected. "The times I've had to hunt for her and found her peeking behind shelving, giggling, playing hide and seek."

"Kids are like that." Agreed Ames. There was a momentary pause.

"Please go on."

"Your wife didn't hang around. Within a couple of minutes, she'd reported Ellen missing and when security drew a blank, we were called in. That would've been within twenty minutes or so."

"No time at all, really." Tom sipped from the teacup. "What happened next?"

"We don't yet know how she was taken. We reviewed the Mall CCTV footage but there was nothing on the tapes we could work with. We really started to worry then, this abduction, or at least that of a child, perhaps any child, rather than Ellen specifically, was clearly planned. Surveillance had been avoided. Routes in and out most likely surveyed. No one saw anything out of the ordinary, anything tangible, frankly, we were stuck."

"How then? I mean, how did you catch them?"

Ames knew how bad this was going to sound and could only imagine the images it was going to throw into Tom's head. But it had to be said.

"The whole thing, the killing and all, it was all filmed, on a mobile phone."

Tom looked up from his cup. Right now, he had no words, there was nothing in his head that could make sense of what he had just heard. Flashes of violence nowadays so commonplace on social media were plucked randomly from his memory and presented as a montage. At the edge of his mind came the realisation that images of Ellen, pixelated scenes of her last physical existence, were now digitised and were never, ever going to go away. Not his imaginings of it, not the hard evidence of it. His daughter was now immortalised. The internet was forever.

"You really shouldn't see it." Ames paused. "There just aren't any circumstances where doing so is going to help you."

Tom's eyebrows knitted. The shot in his tea had begun to dull his finer senses so practicalities were all he could deal with. "Has it gone viral?"

"No. Not for the moment. If it has actually got out, our I.T. has yet to unearth it. Our Intelligence Services have the means to contain data if they act early enough and, in this instance, we've collaborated so their response was swift. Unless we learn otherwise, it's seems that for now, it's been limited to their phones. A small mercy, I think."

Tom nodded. Thankful for what Ames had described as a small mercy. Whatever this footage was, it had been suppressed. Ames sat down next to Tom.

"They were clever, for their age. They appear to have been planning this, or something like it for some time. Their first real mistake was filming it. Somehow, someone at school saw it on one of their phones, and kids being kids, told someone else, who told someone else until teachers called us in. They'd panicked, thought they'd deleted it from their phones, but nothing is ever irretrievable, not these days. Our people recovered the images. There can't be any doubt they did this."

"They? You keep saying they. Who the hell are they?" His voice was even, the expletive purely an expression of frustration.

"Edward and Verity Christian. Twelve years old. Brother and sister. Identical twins, actually."

"And they did this? All of this?" In his detachment, Tom could ask, "Were they pimping for a paedophile?"

"That was one of our first thoughts. But no. The phone evidence is clear. It's them. No doubt. It led us to where we found Ellen, early this morning while you were mid-Atlantic. The twins are in custody. For obvious reasons, I can't tell you where, but I can tell you we can't get a word out of either of them."

"About Ellen?"

"Yes. Ellen. We're struggling with the questioning. Mrs. Christian, the mother, is something of a leading legal light. She's making the process difficult. We're having to dot every 'i' and cross every 't'. We'll get them, but everything about this case, everyone in it, well, it's just a minefield."

Now Tom realised the Press interest. What made Ellen so different from other victims. "You mean my daughter was killed by two twelve-year-olds?"

"We're certain of it." Ames hesitated. Sensing there was more, Tom asked, "And?"

Another pause then Ames continued, his voice lower.

"The reality is that children are occasionally victims of other children and media interest under those circumstances goes off the chart. But these two, this time, it's different. The fact that they're twins. Mummy's a high-flying human rights lawyer and Daddy's something in the City. They're not short of a bob or two." Ames paused again.

"These aren't disadvantaged street kids. Straight A's in school, bright futures predicted and then this…this inexplicable act, but planned, premeditated, deliberate. It's a perfect storm."

"Jesus."

"We could be wrong, but we think it's a unique combination of factors. Twins have killed before, sometimes in partnership but never, as far as I know, have twins so young murdered a toddler. I'm sorry, Mr. Hood, but I have to tell you that the simple reality is that the press isn't about to let go any time soon, if ever. And if that footage ever gets out…"

A Way out

Yesterday was Ellen's birthday. Or rather, it should have been. In another life, we'd have been in the garden. A garden I still remember though I suppose someone else owns it now. It would be mid-August. Shrieking kids would have been abandoned into our care by parents that had left with that sidelong glance that tells you that today is going to be a long day. The summer sun would be beating down and tables heaped with enough E numbers and fizzy drinks to power a small planet, would soon be reduced to a sticky mess. Kids know how to plunder.

Some would be sick. We wouldn't have enough sunblock and the occasional wasp would cause havoc. Yep, she would have been smack in the middle of it all. The birthday girl, Ellen. I get the same memory, year after year. It just doesn't end. It's now 6 years after the event. Ellen would have been nine.

So, there weren't going to be any more birthdays. No Halloween action, no tracking Santa with Norad. It's these memories, and others. The places we'd been, hearing a child's voice. Seeing a stray, solitary, infants' glove in the dirt and the fact that these things catch me when I least expect it…and just won't let me go, that has me here, now. Talking you through my suicide.

I remember that glove quite clearly, the day it was bought and why. We were shopping, the three of us. The cold weather was beginning to creep in and as Ellen was out of her pushchair, it was time to get her something warm to wear. Commercially placed at a child's eye level, the gloves looked like ladybirds. Red wool sporting tiny felt wings with black spots and kind eyes near the fingertips. As the retailer had intended, she'd seen them and fallen in love.

Ellen wasn't a shouter. There were never any tantrums but if she saw something she desperately wanted, she turned those eyes on you. Cornflower blue, irresistibly wide, innocent, and appealing, they were her most potent weapon.

Wearing them straight from the cashier, she meandered around the store, her hands aloft, weaving, making 'ladybird' noises. They were the last thing Sacha had put on her before leaving the house that morning. One of them had led to where her body lay.

When I'm done, just before I'm done, I hope I still have the wit to fire this off to the tabloids. There's been enough media interest in this family to ensure that at least one of them goes to print with it. I don't care if it's compassion, courage or some macabre voyeurism that prompts the editor but for the record, my suicide has a dual purpose.

The first, as already stated, to finally put an end to my misery. I'm stating the obvious there. You don't contemplate ending it all if you're full of the joys of spring. The other, to highlight the fact that those little bastards got out last October. twenty years they said. They've done five. Killers at twelve, convicted murderers at thirteen, and then at eighteen, a year ago, their lives began again. But I want their faces out there. Find them. Get to know them, recognise them in the street, give them no peace. There are people among us who simply shouldn't be. These two qualify.

By ending my suffering, I truly hope that theirs will soon be just beginning. It's up to you to see that it does. I'm unemployed and probably unemployable. The airline stood by me as long as it could. But they had their limits and I'd breached them long ago. They called it a medical release. I didn't argue. The money had run out about the same time as my self-respect.

I have no purpose, no substance. It's time for me to go. I have booze, I have pills and I have an overwhelming sense of failure. An inadequacy stemming from my inability to protect my own.

Too late, I realise that what once seemed so everyday, meant everything to me, and that life without my wife and child makes oblivion a less painful path to tread than tomorrow. I'm not going to bore you with a life history. I know that your interest lies elsewhere. Most of you are already aware of the tragedy that was my family.

Simply accept this. Despite our recent divorce, I love my wife, Sacha. She was my life until guilt decreed otherwise. My daughter, Ellen, has gone. I can think of no other reason to be excused from the burden of carrying on. To those of you that still have something precious; have what once I took less care of than I should, your child or children, I offer this advice. Don't find yourself here. Don't allow a single act of omission, of distraction, of inattention or frustration in the moment to end in destruction and misery.

Anyone reading this who has yet to experience the simple and yet so complicated joy that is parenthood, may never understand. This message is intended for the final group, those that have this thing, this inexpressible responsibility and simply accept it rather than treasure it, those with children and are complacent or naïve enough to believe that they can be left unattended. For when the realisation that you once had these things and suddenly find them gone hits home, simply follow these step-by-step instructions, and meet me somewhere between Hell and Damnation.

The difficult part is having the means. The prospect of stepping in front of a train appalls me. It would have involved traumatising the driver and requires more courage than I possess. The knife held less appeal. That would have involved pain that may well have lasted. I know the pain of the knife. One night, when drunk and insane with vodka and grief I cut myself. Face, arms...I have had enough of pain. I don't like heights. Drowning would have been uncomfortable and Paracetamol, though readily available in quantity, is notoriously unreliable. If found too soon, but too late, it leads inevitably to a slow, pitiful demise involving a massive deterioration of the internal organs, the science of which escapes me. No, to me, a singular coward, the only way was to get hold of some effective but painless means. That required planning.

There is only one way to get hold of a prescription drug. Though you may be suicidal, you need to be able to convince the Doctor that you aren't. You must assume that they are on the lookout for the warning signs and find a way to sidestep their training.

For me, with my story, that was to admit having considered the option of suicide, but to be convincing enough when saying that you believed you had a future. It really isn't that difficult. When contemplating killing yourself, you attempt to deny its necessity by reminding yourself of reasons to live. When talking to a doctor, simply trot out those reasons with sincerity. The real trick is finding the balance. It worked for me. Perhaps the doctor saw through me, but compassion overcame his Hippocratic oath. I don't know and don't care. I have my pills.

The hard part is finding the courage, being able to deny that you might have a future if only you can get through today and tomorrow. The survival instinct is strong, and you need a desperate lack of hope to overcome it. Timing was never an issue. The anniversary was never anything but as low as I could get. But as for actually doing it? All I ever had to do was get the answers to a few simple questions. *Have you really thought this through? Are you absolutely certain that this is what you want? Is Ellen coming back?* When the answers are, *Yes, Yes* and *No*, everything you put into motion all those dreadfully long, hard months ago, falls into place. You have sufficient alcohol to hand to ensure that come what may, you'll be so out of it that you won't care what you stuff into your mouth. All you need to do is get the pills to hand and start drinking.

What makes me different is that having done all that, I'm now telling you about it as I drink. The first bottle of red is almost finished, I estimate that given my increasing ability to absorb alcohol another four or five bottles will be needed before I'm ready. To be on the safe side I actually have nine. My own wine bar. Overkill.

I should tell you it's a Saturday and I stopped writing about 10pm. I think I'm struggling with actually getting on with the job. I'd staggered to the pub, perhaps hoping to find something to cling to, no matter how tenuous. I guess I didn't give it much of a chance because I'm home writing again and it's only 10.35pm, or at least I think it is.

My watch face is kinda hard to read right now. Blurred. Perhaps I wasn't looking for any desperate straws to cling to, simply trying to deny the way this is going to end. Anyway, here I am again, after a couple of vodkas, back into the red wine again.

As I write, I have music on the stereo. I don't want to affect the artist's sales as I have too much affinity with the lyrics so his name will go with me. One day the disc will be carelessly ejected, but not tonight. Not by me. You all have your own musical trigger, a message carried in a song that breaks your heart so insert that into the player and listen as you read.

I stopped smoking a week ago. Tonight, I bought some cigars as giving up seemed like a plan for the future, and kinda pointless. The ashtray I threw away when I quit. I am now using an open window. I exist in a small bedroom, one offered to me by a friend. A friend who remembered enough of the old Tom Hood to take a chance on a peaceful co-existence. I'm sorry, John. I suppose it'll be you who finds this mess.

I'm heavily into the third bottle now and life is taking on a glow. I know this feeling though, these last years of intemperance have taught me that tomorrow does come and irrespective of how rosy life seemed through the bottom of a glass the night before, the pain comes back with the daylight.

The tablets are on top of the TV. I can see them now and am beginning to regard them as a last supper. I have put the CD on continuous play, a track that makes me weep. Cathartic? It doesn't make me feel any better, but I do so enjoy the wallow. I'm looking at my phone too. I do fret about the battery. It's permanently on and never leaves my side. *She might phone you see.* She doesn't. *But she might.*

Four bottles down and five to go. Still lucid but the fingers are slower.

I'll have to hit the spellcheck before I close. The music is playing, and I've opened the pills. Only seven, but good strong ones. To help me sleep. *Thank you, Doctor. Of course, I won't.* Fuck the phone. She's probably asleep anyway. I've taken the tablets.

The reporter from the Telegraph checked first, to be sure that I'd done it. We had a relationship, of sorts. One which developed in the aftermath of the murder and continued sporadically these past years. He'd warn me of stuff likely or due, to be printed. What The Twins were up to. Ask for insight from me on developments, opinions, release dates. I never gave it but knew he had to ask.

He came to the hospital. I was sullen, defeated, uncommunicative. It seems though, that drunk as I was, his was the only address I'd emailed so this story wasn't going to be told. I suppose I should be thankful. Self-pity I'm a cracker at. Being the object of it sat less well.

He was my only visitor. Sacha never came, though in truth; I'd hoped she would. I did hear that she'd thought about it, but that was as far as it went.

Since Ellen's murder and before the divorce, we'd tried so hard not to blame each other. Silent months spent in front of the TV, neither having the courage to begin a conversation that we both knew would end with Ellen and tears. Over time, the silence became commonplace and comfortable, then unbearable. For God's sake, what could we say. *Why did you let go of her hand? Why weren't you here?*

It was all about blame and blamelessness. We had a responsibility to our child and had jointly failed. Now Ellen was dead and all we had left were questions unanswered in the silence. I'd had complete faith and belief in our relationship, in us as a forever entity, never for a moment imagining anything capable of breaking us up but inevitably, like anything that finds itself unable to evolve following a seismic event, our relationship began to wither and die. Now, it was extinct.

Christian

I'd lain there in the hospital bed, wired up to monitors and drips. Resentful and resented. I wasn't supposed to be there. This wasn't a cry for help from someone who'd wanted to be rescued. I'd gone way beyond that point. Rescue was the last thing on my mind. I didn't want to be there, and the nursing staff didn't want me there. Hospital beds were in short supply and for sick people, not sickos. I was largely ignored, no friendly chit chat or cheerful enquiries. Maximum medicine, barely concealed disdain.

That attitude softened slightly when word got around that I was *that* Tom Hood, Ellen's father. That didn't make me feel any better though. It just meant that I'd been in the newspapers again, for another wrong reason.

They kept me in for three days while I was flushed out and interviewed, analysed. The analysis was superficial and felt to me like lip service, an attitude I endorsed. What had led me to attempt suicide? Am I still suicidal? Had I had time to reflect? Desperate to get out of the place, out from under the microscope, I said enough to get me released.

I'd come home from hospital to no home. John had packed my stuff up and I could get it from the garden shed any time I liked. Just don't knock on the door. I couldn't blame him. I left it. There was nothing I wanted or needed. What I needed, was a quiet corner and a drink. I walked into a small hotel and went to the bar. I'd figure out where to doss down later. I ordered, sat myself down, sipped from the first one of the day, and bowed to the inevitable.

Taking my phone from my pocket, I thumbed through the daily must do apps. There was a whole bunch of unchecked emails. The usual bilge. Foreign women desperate for my body. Ugandans with financial offers too good to miss. Not much in way of 'Get Well Soon'. Embarrassed friends, such as I had left, were keeping their distance. Joni Mitchell sprang to mind, *They shake their heads, they say I've changed*. I didn't give a shit. I was the one looking at life from just the one side, mine. I snapped the phone shut and picked up my beer.

"Do you mind if I join you. Mr. Hood?"

I glanced idly upwards, not caring who the interloper was or what they wanted. That changed when I recognised him, Peter Christian, The Father.

Average height, darkish hair greying early at the temple framing an unremarkable face. His expression was solemn. I knew he was early forties, and a banker. Aside from the fact that he'd spawned two murderers, he could have been any man in the street though his clothes looked expensive and probably were. His wristwatch most certainly was. He was carrying a briefcase. That was all I took in.

I focussed back down onto my beer. "What the fuck," I said thickly, darkly, "could you possibly want with me?"

"You won't know unless you allow me to sit."

What the hell. I thought. *Why not?*

I'd seen him a few times before. Once on TV and a few times in the flesh, during the trial. Not feeling much towards any other human being, his presence here meant little to me. That was all over, done and dusted. I didn't have much left in the way of emotion either way so nodded once.

Removing his overcoat and laying it over the back of a chair, Christian put the briefcase on the floor, and sat down.

"We could never have pets, you know." He paused. "We tried once…when they were very young. A puppy. It never reached maturity."

I stayed silent. To be honest, I had no response anyway. Whatever I said would have been meaningless and probably make me appear stupid, so I kept my mouth shut and let him continue.

"That shook me up a little. I didn't quite know how to react, what to do with them. It's been that way ever since. I've lost count of the number of Nannies they had. Each stronger than the last and each unable to bear being near them. We were running out of schools to send them to. They do not mix with others and, well, they're out, you know."

I nodded. "Must be nice." I said.

"I wouldn't know." He replied. "As far as I'm aware, they are with my wife. She and I are separated pending divorce."

He paused to let that sink in. "Allow me to get straight to the point."

His voice and accent were straight out of the 1950's BBC announcer's handbook. I was doing the whole nodding dog thing. I didn't much care what his point was, nor did I care about his problems. I just wanted him out of my face and to get back to my solitary drinking.

"After what happened, yours wasn't the only life that changed…I'm not suggesting that my recent experiences have been in any way on a par with yours, but I need to give you some background."

Nodding dog, again.

"I was, in a sense, an absent father, busy in the City, concentrating on my work and if I'm totally honest, aloof from the process of bringing them up. I'm not a terribly intimate man, never have been and I suppose I could have been considered more of an observer than part of the process. But some things I couldn't help but notice."

"The puppy being one of them?" It seemed to me that a dead pooch stinking up the house should be something you might notice, no matter how distracted you were.

"Indeed…Yes…After that, I took to watching them, the way they interacted, their expressions, things I had perhaps been inconsiderate of, or overlooked before. Watching them grow up or rather, evolve into what they became…even, in a sense, becoming fearful of them or what they seemed capable of, none of that prepared me for what they did."

"To Ellen." A statement. Not a question.

He lost some composure at those words. Her name. He paused briefly, then continued.

"There's something in them Mr. Hood. I'm no psychologist or behaviouralist but they have the ability to unnerve me, to give me an indefinable sense that they aren't ordinary children. They have a fierce intelligence and appear to have no moral boundaries, or at least while they might know where they should be, blithely ignore them. It's as if they know that no matter what they do, I can't simply take them out and shoot them."

That last sentence piqued Tom's interest. Christian wasn't apologising for them or offering excuses. There was bitterness in his words.

"I'd be happy to oblige." I offered, miserably. Then remembered, He'd said *I*, not *we*.

 "And your wife?"

Christian's shrug was almost Gallic.

"I suppose ours was a sort of marriage of convenience, of conformity. We were from the same social sphere, and it seemed like the thing to do. I'm not saying I'm blameless, Mr. Hood, but ours wasn't a union made in heaven. She's a human rights specialist you know. Uncovers, understands, and exploits weaknesses mostly in systems but most profitably in people, something she carries over into her own existence. She even managed to successfully challenge their being held in separate institutions. Unnecessary cruelty, mental hardship, an infringement of some human right or another. Not a care for the rights they deprived your daughter from enjoying…for what they did. If I have any excuse for what has happened, it might be that she understood me a little too well. Try as I might, I can't help but feel that my weaknesses were exposed, and my strengths manipulated. Had I paid more attention, perhaps I'd have seen things a little clearer and none of this would have happened."

Tom had some inkling of what was said. During the trial, he'd seen Mrs. Christian in lawyer mode as part of the defence team. Every harrowing detail of Ellen's ordeal had been listed, discussed; and he made sure he left the courtroom for this, viewed. All of the, *what happened,* none of the, *why's?*

Every legal avenue that could be employed or exploited was brought into play. All of it designed and used for the benefit of their defence and welfare. It had been billed as a 'happy, slappy' incident, a craze that had originated around 2004 in the UK, where random but organised attacks on unsuspecting victims were filmed and shared, that had escalated. So that made it ok then. No it fucking didn't. That presupposes that these attacks are acceptable and a valid defence if it all goes horribly wrong. It also assumes that this was the original intent rather than the prelude to a more premeditated, pitiless, and sinister agenda. A classic case of the legal system being manipulated until the defence compromises and distorts the truth to the point where the simple difference between right and wrong is lost.

"You know about their condition?"

Who didn't? Monozygotic twins. Like the rest of the planet, I'd had to look it up.

Twins abound, identical twins were somewhat rarer, but I'd never even noticed that identical twins were always two boys or two girls, not that I'd ever had contact with any, but it just hadn't occurred to me to even think about it. Before the trial though, I'd had to.

Identical or to give them a scientific definition, monozygotic twins are either XY chromosome, two males or XX, two females, never a boy, girl combination, this is because they form from a single zygote, the zygote being the cell that results when an egg and sperm combine. Identical twins are the result of a single zygote splitting in two instead of remaining a single entity and becoming what will always, always be a pair of girls or boys.

Unless…an anomaly occurs and for some unknown reason, an XY zygote which would normally split and develop into identical twin boys, during the splitting process one twin loses a Y chromosome and develops as a female. It's a genetic mutation. The female may usually, but not always, suffer from Turner Syndrome, this leads to shorter than normal stature and a lack of ovarian development. The female can't reproduce, which in this particular instance, worked for me.

Since records began, depending on whose numbers you believed, there had been less than ten cases where identical twins, sharing exactly the same DNA, had been born as brother and sister. I looked, researched, pored over pages and pages of scientific studies but nowhere, not in one single instance had this mutation resulted in psychotic kids. There were issues, for sure, but they were physical, not mental. But that wasn't how Mrs. Christian had played it.

He took my silence as acknowledgement.

"It was cynical and shameless the way she used that, offering them up as victims somehow suffering their way through life. Unfortunates misunderstood by society and alienated because they are unique. She stage-managed everything. Dressing them, coaching them, ensuring that the one thing no one saw, was a fair trial...blocking anything that might have led to the whole truth. Their guilt was, of course, never in doubt. What she did though, ensured that there would be no adequate punishment. Just, it seems, a few years of education and understanding. Madness. Utter madness." Christian sat, his head shaking slowly from side to side.

I'd seen them in the dock. The Twins. Scrubbed, polished, immaculately presented. Alert and attentive, showing contrition and even managing tears when required. I hadn't believed any of it, neither had the tabloids. Investigative reporters had trawled through The Twins back story. The puppy was news to me but staff that had passed through the Christian household had stories to tell, none of them adding gloss to The Twins CV. But the law can only deal with what's in front of it and how the case is presented.

The verdict was justice, of a sort, the twenty year sentence seemed to reflect that. Subsequent events, The Twins rehabilitation and insertion back into society after only five years...Mrs. Christian had foreseen that. She knew the system alright. It worked for The Twins but in the process, had failed Ellen.

"Do you know she billed me for defending the children?" Christian paused, his voice lowered, as if in shame.

"I paid it and moved out. I haven't been back and have no intention of doing so. Wild horses couldn't drag me back into that asylum. She is a woman who knows the cost of everything and the value of nothing and the children, well...living with them was unnerving, to say the least. I honestly think she saw it as one of her greatest triumphs. The children were not shown to be evil, a threat, as they should have been. She knew their history probably better than I did. They came out of it punished, yes, but not culpable. It wasn't their fault. They were young. It was a prank that went wrong. Unbelievable. Do you know neither of them smoked?"

Tom didn't. The cigarettes and lighter found on the twins were portrayed as their own. They'd used them to torture Ellen. "No. Is that important?"

"Think about it, Mr. Hood. They don't smoke. There was only one purpose in taking cigarettes with them...to inflict harm. Knowing just that tiny detail would have changed people's perception of events. There was so much more that she was able to neutralize or have removed from evidence." Christian let that sink in.

"Your wife knew about the cigarettes?"

"Of course. Yet she couldn't see beyond the need to show them in a false light, even if it meant hiding what we both knew to be a basic truth. Their actions were inhuman, they are inhuman, yet she found a way to deflect opinion away from that simple fact. I can say with some certainty that they planned it, they did it and it's my belief they don't for a single moment regret it. To them, the gratification was what it was all about, and they are older now, wiser, less naïve and if anything, more calculating than ever. They're not going to change; I don't believe they would if they could. Today, the risk of them doing something similar, well, that risk doesn't simply remain, it's heightened."

He left the sentence hanging. 'I'm just going to get myself a drink. Would you like one?"

Head nod again. Beggars can't be choosers. In anticipation, I drained my pint while waiting for the fresh one. My guess is that this interlude was orchestrated to elicit some thoughtful response from me. I didn't have one. When he returned with the drinks, I raised mine in acknowledgement and waited him out.

"Some days ago, Mr. Hood, I received a visit."

I looked across at him, his tone had gone from the matter of fact to one tinged with sadness, perhaps even a hint of fear.

"My doorbell rang. I don't often get visitors, I've led a solitary lifestyle of late and don't advertise my whereabouts, in fact I can't recall having heard the doorbell before. Any meetings I have tend to be by appointment and off piste, so to speak...It was them, the children. With hindsight, I'm grateful that I didn't invite them in."

He had my attention now, I'd not had a first-hand account of them since the trial and was curious to know what, if anything, had changed.

"There were niceties at first. You might even have imagined that it would have been some kind of tearful reunion, but something told me this wasn't so. As I said, Mr. Hood, I've grown wary of them."

"And?"

"It seems I was justified. I'm really not very good at pretence and my reluctance to engage with them at any level was, it seems, quite apparent. Once the smiles dropped, any notion that this was a social visit was soon dispelled. They'd come for money. Their inheritance, they called it. They didn't even give me the benefit or courtesy of making it a request. Once the preamble was over and they'd seen my reaction to them simply being there, it swiftly developed into demanding money with menaces, to paraphrase legal jargon...I have a week, it seems, to put things right, as it was put to me."

He paused, taking a drink. This seemed to settle him, and he continued.

"That isn't going to happen, Mr. Hood. I gave them some assurances and what little cash I had in the house simply to get rid of them but the kind of money they want from me...well, I simply can't empower them that way. They are young adults now. Bigger, stronger, much cleverer, even artful, perhaps craftier might best describe them. No, they'll get nothing from me."

He let that thought hang in the air before changing tack.

"More often than you might imagine, financial investors require the use of professional security services. Prior to winding up my firm, I'd had occasion to invest in unstable or even unsavoury regimes or individuals. It's quite normal. But risk assessment and monitoring aren't something within the purview of financial institutions, which is when you call upon such organisations. As a general rule, these are ex-servicemen. SBS and Royal Marines to deal with piracy and the like, SAS for exotic locations and personal protection. I have two of the latter with me now. One drives me, the other follows. Not cheap but comforting, to say the least. They are outside now, one at each entrance, apparently. I leave the practicalities to them. They've been with me since that visit."

My surprise was evident. I glanced at the one door in my eyeline but couldn't see anyone. "You feel that The Twins are that much of a threat?"

"I don't just feel it, Mr. Hood. I know it. Deep in my bones I know it." He sat quietly for a moment before continuing. "You've lost your job?"

I resented what seemed to me to be an intrusion. "I think, Mr. Christian, you already know the answer to that."

"Yes. Yes, I do." He paused while he took a quiet drink from his glass. Red wine, I noted.

"You are owed more than an apology, Mr. Hood. Nothing I could say or do will ever express my horror, revulsion, or deep sadness regarding what happened." Christian paused briefly. "But I had to do something and once I'd thought deeply about what that should be, it seemed to me that there really was only one thing I could do, given my abilities in specific areas."

Another pause, while he drank from his glass.

"Over the years, I have, in one way or another, made a great deal of money. Since the incident, I ceased trading...at least professionally, closed my offices and have been slowly liquidating my assets. My car is leased. I no longer own my own home. I rent."

"Comfortably, I suppose." I said, a trace of sarcasm evident in my tone.

"Quite." He replied, unmoved. Making money was his business. He was, I'd heard, very good at it. The conversation had moved from the personal to the professional and his confidence had returned.

"Currently. One of my accounts has in excess of fourteen million pounds available. Most of it cash on deposit."

"Lucky you. So?" I queried.

His next words were, to say the least, something of a surprise. It was a good job I wasn't drinking from my beer at the time, we'd have both been wearing it.

"Half of that is yours. Yours to do whatever you want with. Available immediately."

While maths isn't my strong point, it only took a fraction of a second for the figure to hit home.

"Seven million quid?" I had to work hard to get the words out.

"Plus some change." He replied, evenly.

"I don't want it." I have no idea why I said that. Perhaps my instant reaction was that it was blood money. Either way, I said it, despite the rush of adrenalin those figures had created.

"I thought you might say that." Christian replied softly.

"But you don't have a great deal of choice I'm afraid." He continued.

"After what the children did, I knew that I had to do something to make amends. I couldn't change the past, but I could help to change the future." He paused, steepling his fingers.

"Everything I've done from then to now was with that in mind. When I closed down my firm, I opened another, more private affair, with you as a partner. Over the course of the last five years, we've done very well." He paused again, his voice dropping.

"I know what happened recently, Mr. Hood, your hospital visit. I was hoping for a nice round figure but now would seem to be the most opportune time to step in, as it were. I'm exceptionally good at what I do Mr. Hood. I know about money, how to make it and how to make it grow but most importantly, how to do it legally. This money is clean, it's yours, and it's the least I can do. Additionally, in the event of my demise…accidental or otherwise, my full estate is bequeathed to a foundation I've been busy setting up. One thing is absolutely certain, my children will never inherit a single penny. You'll find a copy of my will in here."

He picked up the briefcase and set it down by my feet.

"Everything you need to know is inside. As I said, Mr. Hood, it's up to you what you do with it. You can give it away or carry on doing what you're doing and try drinking it. Good luck with that."

Christian stood and picked up his cashmere overcoat.

"You'll find a mobile phone in there." Christian nodded at the briefcase.

"There's only the one number on it, the security firm. It will be answered day or night, and they don't observe holidays. As you now know, my divorce is imminent. At some point in the future, all of my financial details must be declared to my wife or her representatives, unfortunately, that will include our brief partnership and your share in it. I hadn't anticipated the children's visit or their aggressive demands. Had I done so, perhaps I'd have been less candid when setting the business up. This money may cause you some problems, Mr. Hood, problems I hadn't foreseen. When my wife becomes aware of what I've done, it would be wise to assume the children will know shortly after. They may well feel a certain sense of entitlement, of having been cheated. If they get that into their heads, then there is a degree of risk in simply being you. With that in mind, I've taken the liberty of giving my security contacts your details, or at least, those I have. The mobile is a direct link to them. Clearly, given recent events, they already know something about you and have indicated a willingness to help. Should you feel the need, I urge you to call them." Christian walked towards the exit.

"I doubt that I'll see you again, Mr. Hood. I'm booked to fly out this afternoon."

"Where to?" Tom asked, with too much on his mind to think of anything else to say.

"Somewhere peaceful, quiet, restful. Somewhere as far away from this country as I can get. We're both entering a new beginning, Mr. Hood. I'd try to make the best of it if I were you."

Something surfaced in my mind. An old, impossible idea. As he was leaving, I expressed it. "What if I decide to go after them?"

Christian turned at the door and with an inscrutable expression looked Tom square in the eye.

"The world won't miss them, Mr. Hood." He paused, as if for effect and then continuing slowly out said softly, "Neither will I."

The door closed behind him, ending the meeting.

God knows how long I sat there, the briefcase a mute reminder of a surreal half an hour. Remembering what was supposed to be in it, the keys to seven million quid, I hooked it over with my foot and nestled it beneath my chair.

That wasn't enough, I needed to see inside and so leaned down and pulled it onto my lap. Snapping open the locks, I opened it. On top of a bunch of paperwork I saw the mobile. Picking it up, I checked the contacts list. Just the one number. Christian's spooks. It was fully charged.

Putting that to one side, further rummaging revealed papers, statements, and the like, I started to study. I probably only took ten minutes but at first glance, they bore out everything Christian had said. It was there, a shade over seven million pounds sterling. In a variety of accounts, all bearing my name. In the lid of the briefcase, in tailor made pockets, were a variety of credit cards, again bearing my name.

I matched them to accounts in the paperwork and saw my credit limit. I swallowed. Not thinking too hard about the morality of accepting this largesse I stood, unsteadily, it must be said, went to the front desk and checked myself in. Going up to my room, the first and only thing I did, was to hit the minibar.

Daylight streaming through the open curtains woke me. I made to get up but fell back, my head throbbing. My mouth tasted like a baby dragon had crawled in and taken a shit in it and I struggled momentarily to remember where I was and how I'd got here. Given yesterday's drama, my memory lapse didn't last long. Christian. Seven million quid. I tried to snap awake, but my hangover defeated me. Thick tongued, I ordered breakfast brought up and clambered gingerly off the bed.

The erstwhile contents of the minibar were strewn around me and testament to the ache in my head that sharpened painfully with every movement. I made it to the shower without puking and ten minutes later, felt and smelt a little more human. Breakfast arrived.

I'd ambitiously requested a full English, all I managed was the tea and toast. I ordered a second pot of coffee and thought hard about what to do next or more to the point, what to do now. What had Christian said? Give it to charity or piss it up the wall. I hoped I'd do neither. That had hurt, rankled. I felt judged.

Christian's third option, to make the best of it, appealed to me from somewhere back in time. The mania that all but consumed me the first few weeks after Ellen's murder.

If I'd seen them in the street, I'd have mowed them down by train, car, pitchfork, machine gun, without a second thought. Kidnap. Murder. Hot revenge. That rage was frustrated though. Once arrested, that was it.

Until recently, to the best of my knowledge, they hadn't been on any street anywhere. There had been no opportunity to act hastily. Thoughts of how to put the money to best use went through my mind. Most of them not pretty, some, impractical, fanciful. One stuck out like a sore thumb. That in this day and age, the first rule of criminal law enforcement appears to be to follow the money, which I now had in abundance. I'd have to be careful. Very, very careful. On the other hand, suicide was now off the table. For the first time in a very long time, I felt the faint stirrings of optimism.

Changeling

There's a sense of helplessness that goes with being part of a high-profile incident. Everything you say and do has a habit of finding its way onto someone's desk. Reporter, Social Worker, Case Officer, Policeman. You are under a variety of microscopes, some of them official. Much of the time, they are way ahead of you, history has a habit of repeating itself and if you have any ideas based on retribution…and believe me there isn't one of them that doesn't go through your mind, they already have experience of it.

Time is the only way to get distance from these people. You're never really off the radar, but there's always the next big thing that shuffles you further into the shadows. The trick is not to put yourself back into the light. Let events overtake you, let the next big news story shunt you out of the picture. Be grey.

I'd fucked up a bit with the whole suicide thing. Every man and his dog wanted his piece of that, but that was then, this, six months later, was now. I had purpose and a plan. The substance of which was to get to the Twins before, as Christian suggested they might, they got to me, that was as far as it went.

All I knew for certain was that I wasn't prepared to assume they'd leave me alone, not when they had seven million reasons not to. I'd have to let that evolve as a series of problems that needed to be solved. My first problem had been to sober up and start thinking straight again.

I'd kept quiet about the money. But keeping quiet about it didn't mean that news of it wasn't going to be out there. Once Christians divorce went through, interested parties trawling through the detail were certain to spot a partnership with my name attached to it. It crossed my mind they'd come looking for me but lying in wait and setting traps didn't sit well. There was no control there and I didn't like surprises. Giving some thought to what Christian had said, about a week after our meeting I fired up the spook phone. It was answered on the third ring.

"Yes, Mr. Hood?"

I wasn't sure what I'd expected. Phone anyone these days and you have to run through the whole data protection rigmarole, your birthday, first line of your address, suit size, postcode and your mobile number which clearly, you're actually calling them on. Maddening. But this was refreshing. Either they didn't have many clients, or the mobile had brought my name up on a computer screen somewhere.

It was a woman's voice, alert and on the ball. My prepared speech crumbled in the face of such efficiency, so I ad-libbed.

"So, you know me, but I don't know you. What do I call you?"

"Daniels will do." She replied, business-like. "How can we help?"

"Is that first or last?" I persisted.

Silence…then, "How can we help?"

I mentally shrugged. Whatever kind of 'receptionist' she was, she'd clearly had the training. I hoped Christian had given them the full skinny on the Twins so just went for it.

"I'd like my ex-wife to be given full protection. Is that something you can help me with?"

"Of course, Mr. Hood. We have some understanding of your situation and the threat. We have her address. Leave it with us. We'll contact you if there are any issues."

I fumbled for a bit. I didn't want them to think I wanted a proxy stalker. Sacha had a life, and I didn't want to interfere with that. "You know why I'm requesting this?"

"We do. Your sponsor gave us a full briefing. You have a twin problem. As does he. Is Sacha aware or would you prefer covert cover?"

Jesus, they were way ahead of me. Sacha's name, her address, all at their fingertips. As for my sponsor, a 'he', with a twin problem, it could only have been Christian.

"No, she doesn't know anything, and I'd like it to stay that way."

I blabbed on a bit about it doesn't matter what it costs and gave her an account number to draw on.

After that call, I'd kept myself to myself, stayed quiet, and dropped out of society. You can do that if you have the wherewithal. And I had plenty of that. Temporarily, I'd moved most of it to my personal account. If I'm honest, just to establish that it really existed and actually belonged to me. The bank had been much more helpful than when my account had been the wrong side of balanced. With that in mind I told them that on this occasion, I was unable to help them with their application and instead, just spread it around where it could come to the least harm and was readily available.

Useful stuff, money. Since Christian's intervention I'd quietly gone about the business of staying off the drink and making some repairs to what Tom Hood had been. I did some stuff for Sacha too. I bought her a house and a funky little convertible.

Not knowing, I'd supposed she'd rented somewhere after I'd left our family home. It's what I would have done, and I wanted her to have some roots. The car was easy. She'd always had a thing about the Porsche Speedster, think James Dean and you can picture it. I knew she could handle it; this was a girl who understood a manual choke and double de-clutching. But that might have led her to thoughts of me and I couldn't have that. I got her a Boxster instead.

I'd had quite a pleasant, out of body few weeks, car buying, enhancing my wardrobe and house hunting. It was almost as if life were normal, if somewhat enriched. I'd found the perfect place, one that had been our idea of where we'd like to live if only we could afford it. Not exactly your rose covered cottage but something quite like it. A lawyer I knew assured me he could find her, give her the keys and deeds without my name being mentioned, and mumble something about a philanthropic gesture from a sympathiser. *Don't ask too many questions Dear. Just take them.* It was the least I could do. I called the spooks and gave them her new address. They already had it; these guys were The Jedi.

My face was well known due to tabloid appearances, but that was Tom Hood the airline exec. I needed a new one. I took the time to grow my hair, which I darkened.

Stopped shaving, adopted tinted glasses, changed my wardrobe and car, and bought a nice, isolated, little place of my own close enough to my hometown; *you never know, she might call*, but far enough away to avoid old haunts, memories or being recognised. It had everything I needed right down to a cellar, small gym, a good-sized pool, and privacy. It was where Tom Hood would register for the Doctor, the Dentist and where his mail would go.

Years back, I'd picked up a dodgy hip playing rugby and hadn't been able to get it sorted as time off from work wasn't an option. Now though, I'd gone private. Scraping my late thirties, I was as good as I was going to get. The hip was fixed, and the limp had gone. The Twins were young and fit and were certain to be better movers than me. The gym and the surgeons had levelled the playing field a little. I'd packed in the fags. Aside from the obvious health benefits I wasn't going to be making anybody a gift of my DNA via a carelessly discarded dog end.

The gun was going to be more of a problem, and I absolutely knew I needed one. It was time to find out how resourceful I'd become, or not. I'd been a Reservist for a while. My service had seen me out in Bosnia. Mundane logistics stuff in Banja Luka but I did know which end of a gun was the dangerous one.

I also knew what I wanted. I'd carried one and there was a comfort in having a Browning Hi Power strapped to your hip. If you had to use it, and you hit what you were aiming at, whatever it was wasn't going to get up again.

But this was modern day Britain. Since Dunblane in 1996, pretty much anything that went bang was either completely banned, de-activated, or needed a licence. I wasn't going to be able to stroll into a gun shop and pick up a 9mm. Nor did I have a Hollywood button in the bedroom which when pressed, would cause a wall to swish back revealing an arsenal kept for moments just like this, when my hidden but very special abilities could be brought reluctantly back into play. No trapdoor, no puff of smoke, no sliding drawers, no hidden talents. I didn't have any dodgy mates. That left just the one choice and to be truthful, it was one I fancied. I had to *know* how far I could go, whether I could see this thing through.

All my life suburbia had sheltered me from society's underbelly but that didn't mean I was unaware of its existence. Folks like me either ignored or kept away from feral Britain, but it was out there, and I had as much time as it took to burrow in. More to the point, I didn't want a trail leading back to me. I was about to go undercover. Whatever that meant.

I wasn't trained for it. I had huge doubts about my ability, or lack of it, to carry it off. On the plus side, I reckoned I had two assets. The money was the big thing. It gave me options, the best of which was that I didn't need to work, that gave me the time to train my other asset. I had a brain; it was time to use it for something other than as an instrument of self-torture.

Recently, following internet advice, I'd set up a box in there, one with a tight lid I could screw down, like a coffin. Years ago, when these things mattered, I'd rescued an old, Victorian blanket box from a bonfire, restored it, stencilling coloured balloons and the word 'Toybox' on it. It used to sit at the foot of Ellen's bed. Now it existed only in my head and in it, I lodged the memories that had been crippling me these past years. From time to time, an image would escape but, as the exercise grew in strength, so did my ability to keep the thoughts and pictures caged. As the months wore on, if one slipped through a crack, it became easier; not easy, but easier, to crack open the lid of the box and quickly shove it back in. This was self-help on a dramatic scale.

I began to feel human again. I became more focussed, found it easier to absorb new ideas. I spent hours on the internet or immersed in books, mostly spy stuff, trying to build a new way of thinking. It wasn't as if there was a course I could enrol in, so remote research and learning was the best I could do. I hoped it was enough.

The Hole

I took to studying demographics. A city was no good, the police would be far too organised and aware. Towns with suburbs were out as well. Outraged citizens have a habit of opposing licences for seedy bars. Nope, I needed something a little different and picked an urban overspill.

Throughout the UK, huge developments, begun in the 60's and expanded through to the 90's, had seen some old market towns become less salubrious than their histories deserved as populations doubled. But such was progress, and it was one of these that suited my purpose. Policing was overstretched and they kept their conviction rate up by nailing motorists and drunks. Sometimes simultaneously. You had to be really stupid to get caught with drugs or guns. The police knew they were there all right, but stings and convictions needed organisation, numbers, which cost too much and took too long. So, they just waited and hoped until something criminally juicy fell into their lap.

After taking up a quiet residence, it had taken a few weeks of pub hopping, listening, sitting quietly with a pint and a crossword, in shirt and tie, a worker taking an hour out before going home at the end of the day, to uncover the less wholesome taprooms.

It didn't look like much from the outside, a three-storey frontage with blacked out windows and a double door for an entrance but The Hole in The Wall stood head and shoulders above anything else for the kind of reputation I was looking for. Smackheads and dopers in the week, a row of motorcycles at the weekend. If I was going to find cocaine anywhere, it was here. And where there's cocaine, if the tabloids were anything to go by, there were guns.

If it all went horribly wrong, if I slipped up through lack of experience or knowledge, I could always bug out, run away. There were lots of little towns out there, all of them just what I was looking for. I had patience, time was on my side and if I had to, I could start again. Time to ditch the shirt and tie.

It wasn't difficult. Find a shitty little flat. Pay cash six months in advance to an Asian guy who was more interested in the money than me, less paperwork, no tax. Adopt jeans and hoodie and daily, around noon, mooch into town, order a beer, sit down with a laptop and ask about wifi. Everywhere has it now, even a dump like The Hole. Be quiet and if you make it regular, sooner or later people get curious.

By letting little gems out to the bar staff, it was soon general knowledge that I was a single guy, living locally who bought and sold cars on the internet. I was no fan of Revenue and Customs and enjoyed a beer. Within a fortnight, I'd done my first favour and with the kind of cash I had behind me, it made no difference if I made or lost on the car deal. I watched for a while and soon enough, clocked the guys with fast hands making their drops to their regular customers.

Tentative enquiries got me my first gram of coke. Having made the connection, I'd buy more or less on a daily basis. I had to practice how to take it, referring to movies for the standard method.

It took a bit of getting used to and I'd spend nights in the flat spaced out while still trying to think straight but over a week or so, felt confident enough to go public. If you buy it, you have to be seen using it. Occasionally, I'd even share it. Doing cocaine is like a ritual. The tension of making the deal; cash slipped into a hand or tucked into a pocket, the bag in return. Huddling with a mate cutting the lines on a toilet cistern. Rolling the twenty. This is rock star territory. Trust isn't really that hard to build when you're breaking the rules in company.

Over time, I became part of the furniture and, now and then, even got high fived when out and about. I always had enough cash but not too much. No one cared how I made my money, just that I spent it. I'd talk about a few hundred here and there on this car or that and if a deal, fictional or not, was particularly beneficial, spread a little happiness around a growing clique. You just have to do all this kind of thing gently. Watch for tripwires, but gradually get involved in the occasional vodka frenzy and be one of the guys. In time, that's what you are.

Inside six months, I had two burn phones. One for the drugs, the bash phone in local speak, and one for day-to-day crap. They were never going to be registered, had nothing in them that even sniffed of Tom Hood, no photos, no names, nothing. Electronic trails can really fuck you up and I'd checked the best way to see it didn't happen to me. Forget fancy encrypted gizmos. The most secure phone is one bought with cash, sim only and nothing personal in it knowing that you are quite happy to toss it in the trash. Think The Matrix. Never, ever use it for the web.

For the time being I was Tom Hamilton. I expected the occasional *Don't I know you?* but these days bore only a passing resemblance to old, vague, tabloid photos of a dead kids Dad, and, as he and I were worlds apart, I figured it was something I could easily shrug off with the doppelganger theory. As it was, it never happened, and I stopped worrying about it.

I knew who was growing weed and where, even the varieties, AK47, BC Bud, if they were organic or hydro. These guys loved to talk. After a while, I was helping out with regular watering and feeding and before I knew it, I had my own grow. Nothing big, just half a dozen plants, kinda establishing my credentials and getting me further in.

The coke dealers were my mates, before long, I was hovering around their suppliers. It's a natural thing. From the soft stuff, weed, pills, dealing coke is the next step up the ladder. I can't say my head was clear all the time, but I'd been at this for a while now and was, if you like, a changed man. I didn't think too hard whether I cared about that or not, if there were time later, I'd think about it then. I never talked about my past.

Initially, this made me suspect but as time went on, it gave me a subtle mystique and earned me a reputation as a man who could keep his mouth shut. Any ideas that I might be some undercover policeman, were soon dropped. There was no way I could break the law on the scale I was and be a nark. I didn't think too hard about the consequences of what I was doing. I had one objective, and this seemed the best way to achieve it.

Cynically, I reckoned that given who I was and how my life had changed I had little doubt that if caught, there was a good chance of a sympathetic judge. So, I kept going. I even had my own special buddy, Pete. Recently divorced, he was maybe ten years younger than me; or so his fucking awful taste in music suggested. I never asked and he never said, and was partying his way through the rough end of twenty grand, which was his share of the house he and his ex had sold when their ways had parted. 5'10", good looking, fit and solid, Pete hadn't a care in the world and figured that he'd worry about the cash running out when the time came and not before, he even said as much.

We hung together because we were both newbies, Pete landing in town about a fortnight before I had. He'd occasionally crash at my place, we'd share booze, coke, and breakfast. Not girls though. Pete was the life and soul, and the ladies liked him. I had a few years on the girls, Sacha on my mind and as I showed no interest, wasn't pursued.

Most of them were coke whores. But not in the way you might imagine that strikes you. It didn't seem to matter to them who or what they were in their everyday lives but when the sun went down and at weekends, the office clothes got discarded and the secretaries, PA's, nurses, single Mum's and shop workers were on the town, dressed to kill in their LBD's and looking to party. It was common knowledge that The Hole was the party place. Particularly once the doors were locked after hours and the unknown punters sent on their way.

After closing, the place built quickly, almost ritually into what can only be described as a Speakeasy. The ashtrays would come out of hiding and there was no need to find somewhere private to do your nose powder. Spirit measures were discarded in favour of the Continental freehand pour and the music cranked up. The Hole didn't give a shit once the doors were locked and I have to say, every once in a while, it was fucking brilliant, usually lasting until the last man fell off his stool. It explained the blacked-out windows.

There were drawbacks of course, mostly the psychos. That breed I tried to avoid. But avoiding them isn't the same as having to put yourself in close proximity which was occasionally necessary. Apparently, they had their uses, but they were mad, brooding fuckers that I didn't know how to deal with. They were dangerous because they were low brow morons, unpredictable and stupid. Every town has at least one. But this place bred them.

All human life and lowlife inhabited The Hole, surreal doesn't come close. Clothes, hair, colour, creed, religion or politics, none of that mattered, a cosmopolitan paradise. Oddly though, some of the guys scattered amongst the dealers, growers, thieves, and users were ok, likeable, charismatic even. They just were what they were. What they did was a lifestyle choice and a few of them had done time for it but in the main, they were just looking out for themselves, not considering any harm that might come from it.

You can judge me on this, but I didn't see how that made them any different to Politicians or Bankers. In it for themselves. Just like them. Just like me.

I was six months in and lately, I'd been asked to help out with a few small things. Unload a truck in the dead of night. Move some coke around. No major dramas but I was getting closer to the bad boys. Figures on the periphery now had names. Some of those names would acknowledge me around the bars. One Friday night, Pete and I strolled into The Hole and on seeing us, the barman gestured behind him with a thumb.

Behind the bar, a dimly lit corridor led to a glass wash area, storage rooms and at the far end a small, corner office. It was furnished with a filing cabinet, shelving carrying paperwork, small boxes and random defunct beer tap clips. On a battered desk stood a PC monitor, a grubby, well used keyboard, unfiled receipts, a calculator, and a biscuit tin, one of those big, square ones you see around at Christmas. Behind the desk, in a Captain's chair, sat the owner of The Hole in The Wall, Kyle Goodman, known as Benny, I figured because of a fondness for Benzedrine, there being no Jazz on the jukebox.

Local boy done good by being bad. I'd heard rumours of armed robberies being bandied about. Skinny, sallow skinned, dark thin hair pulled back in a ponytail and sporting the mandatory goatee. His favoured clothing, unrelieved black. Biker boots, jeans, t-shirt topped off with a plain, black leather waistcoat.

Me and Benny had been getting along fine these past months. His were the trucks I unloaded, the drugs I moved, the guy I did favours for. We'd had deep, meaningful chats. Along with Pete and a few others, I was one of his boys. On his right, loomed Joey. A massive knuckle dragger who Benny rarely went anywhere without. Apparently too big to be of much use in a fight, but I'd been told he was handy with a knife and had no qualms about using one. I stood next to Pete, and we watched Goodman snort a line of coke. Finishing with a flourish, he looked up at us and gestured at a couple of lines on the tabletop.

"Help yourselves, guys."

It would have been rude not to so Pete and I stooped and took it through a couple of rolled up twenties.

There was the usual second or two of snuffling and nostril checking and Goodman let this subside before speaking again, staccato.

"Fuckers've had me over. I can't have it. And blatant with it."

He kept his voice low, there was a bar full of rockers not a million miles away. Me and Pete knew better than to interrupt. Goodman liked an audience.

"I want it back, 2 kilos, straight out of Escobar's back pocket." This meant it was uncut. Or at least, as uncut as it was likely to be by the time it got to Goodman.

Let me give you some figures here. On the street, a gram goes for £60 or thereabouts. There are 28 grams in an ounce, give or take, and 35 ounces in a kilogram. Don't blame me for how this bastardised system became common, it comes down to manufacturers supplying in metric and the U.S. dealers using pounds and ounces. So, a fucked-up kilo is 1,120 grams, give or take. You turn that into money by multiplying by £60. Roughly 70 grand. But that's before you bash it. You can cut the stuff with Benzocaine or Phenacetin. Both look the same and give the same numbing effect. A great marketing idea but both traceable and hard to come by unless you buy the cheap stuff, £12 a kilo but mixed in a Chinese bathtub and therefore dodgy in the extreme.

Glucose or Powder Protein is another option, looks the part but with no numbing characteristics. But whatever agent the basher chooses or can find, once cut; depending on which pusher it's destined for, he'll measure it out into their preferred weight. This then gets shoved under a pneumatic press turning it into a glistening hard block of 'pure' coke which when broken down again, results in a powder that has all the characteristics of the real thing. Anything but.

So, do the math. Goodman had 2 kilos of 'pure'. If he was lucky, very lucky, this might be up to 70% coke. He'll turn that into eight kilos. To him, that's half a million, give or take. Incidentally, by the time that gets to you, your friendly neighbourhood dealer, and the guy above him would have cut it again, I don't know what with but it 'aint gonna be wholesome. If you get 3% coke in your little baggy, you'll be doing well.

"Half a million quid." He growled. "I want it back."

That was Goodman. The numbers mattered to him. It was how he measured himself. I let Pete do our talking. I'm the quiet guy, remember? Pete spoke.

"Who's got it?"

Goodman cut three more lines. Took one and invited us in. We rolled our twenties, bent, and snorted.

"Those Peabody fuckers I reckon."

Peabody's. My second choice of bar when making my selection. Sartorially more elegant than The Hole but, until now at least, more weed dealers than coke. They were at the other end of town.

We had the bikes; they had the jazzed up hot hatches, Ford Asbo's, Vauxhall Ashtrays, Scooby Doo's. There was rarely any contact between the ends of the spectrum.

"How?" Pete again.

"Last night, on the Motorway services. Same way we always get it. Fast Johnny was doing the pick-up. He'd checked it, paid up and the supplier had gone. That made it mine. Fuckers beat the shit out of him, nicked the coke and were on their toes."

"And we think it's Peabody's because?"

"Johnny had clocked one of their motors parked up on his way in. Didn't think much of it 'cos you see 'em around all the time. When he woke up it was gone. And so was my coke."

I spoke for the first time. "A bit thin, isn't it?"

"It's enough." Goodman growled. "They've been close to treading on my toes for a while. Figured they'd upgrade. It's time they were reminded who runs this zoo. So, right now I really don't care if it was them or not, I 'aint happy and someone's gonna pay. We'll start with them. See what happens when we shake the tree. I want that fuckin' coke back."

He reached for the biscuit tin and levered off the lid. I heard rustling and his hand emerged with a robust, plastic shopping bag, ironically as it turned out, a 'bag for life'. He put it on the desk. It clunked heavily with a solidity I recognised.

"You 'aint the only ones on this but I don't wanna go out mob handed. You'll work in pairs. 'Til now, the Police don't really give a shit about us or them, as long as we aint outrageous."

Benny looked straight at me. "You were Army?" That had been one of our deep, meaningful conversations.

I nodded. "Reserve but spent some time in the shit."

"Then you'll know how to use one of these."

He pushed the bag at us. "Take 'em and you're in...all the way in. There's a finder's fee. Don't take 'em and you can fuck off and not come back." He waited looking straight at us.

This was the moment of truth and there could be no backing out. It didn't matter what Goodman wanted. What I wanted was there, right in front of me, on the table. I tried not to appear mad keen on the idea of picking it up.

"Do they work?" I asked.

"They did the last time they had a day out. They're clean and loaded. Full mags. Don't be stupid. Don't get caught. Get my coke."

Pete opened the bag and took out two semi-automatic pistols. I couldn't tell what brand but at first glance, they looked in good order. I'd heard rumours of armed robberies. Perhaps they weren't just rumours after all. Pete handed me mine and I tucked it into the waistband of my jeans, in the small of my back, hiding it with the hem of my hoodie. I had my gun. Time to get the fuck out of Dodge.

Leaving The Hole in The Wall, I told Pete I needed to get back to the flat for some spare clothes. This made sense, if we got bloody, we'd need clean gear to change into. We agreed to meet back here in an hour. That was all the time I needed. I drove straight to the flat. All I wanted, was my laptop. Everything else was Tom Hamilton's crap. Not mine. There were half a dozen, well, five now, guys out there with guns looking to do some damage. If this kicked off as badly as I thought it might, local motorists were going to catch a break. The law were going to be all over this and if a name came up, it would be Hamilton, not Hood.

They'd need forensics or a crystal ball to track me down and hopefully, I'd either kept under the police radar or wouldn't matter enough to be hunted. Benny didn't have forensics or a fortune teller. I left the flat without a backward glance. All that was necessary to be done here, was done.

I walked a very twitchy mile or so in the dark to a small lock up on the edge of town. It was here I kept my clean car. A big, fat, silver Mercedes. A businessman's car, nondescript but a debadged AMG powerful enough to get me out of trouble if I needed to throw my weight around. It was time to go home.

I pulled slowly out of the lock up, lights off. Leaving the car running, I got out and pulled down the shutter for the final time. When the rental cash ran out, it'd be someone else's. A quick eyeball showed no activity or interest nearby. I slid quietly back into the Merc. I had an hour's drive ahead of me, most of it on dual carriageways or motorways.

Easy access and egress had been a priority on my search for a town with a gun in it, country roads, picturesque as they are, can be a bitch. The motorway was quiet, with just a hint of roadworks and with the dark outline of trees framing a pewter night sky, the Merc thrummed along with me in its cocoon.

With luck, I'd be home about 2am. I was conscious that being stopped for anything would be disastrous with what I was carrying.

Looking, and very probably smelling, the way I did wasn't typical of the average Merc owner. I'd be looked at hard if I got pulled over. I needed to get back into Tom Hood's skin. That said, against my instincts, I kept my speed at just above the limit.

Thirsty for coffee, I resisted the impulse to stop and in time, my junction came up and I slipped smoothly onto the exit ramp. Roadside lamps, roundabouts and speed cameras slowly gave way to school signs and habitation, signs of life eased as I neared home, then petered out completely. A couple of minutes down a hedgerowed lane and I'd made it. The car was recognised, and the gate swung open automatically. Passing through I watched in my rear-view mirror as it closed shut.

Gravel crunched beneath the Mercs tyres until ahead, my headlights illuminated the main house. More sensors spotted me and raised the garage door. Once inside, it closed behind me, and the overhead lights came on. Switching off the car, I sat there, listening. The hot engine ticked occasionally as the Merc settled but that was it. The place was utterly silent.

I had good reason to hangfire for a minute or two. I was no gardener, and the house had ample lawns and decorative gardens in the grounds. An old boy, Sid, took care of all that twice a week and I needed to be sure he'd kept to his brief and that the house was nice and empty.

I gave it a couple of minutes, but the silence was constant. No unwelcome guests.

I realised I was sweating. Time to get out of character. Deactivating the security system, I opened the interconnecting door to the house, closed it behind me then leaned against it, still sweating, catching my breath. I took the pistol from my waistband and shoved it in a drawer. I'd have a proper look at my trophy tomorrow.

There was no milk, so I had to take my coffee black. Catching my reflection in the mirror reminded me too much of Hamilton. I stripped, threw Hamilton's clothes in the bin, took a hot shower, and had the luxury of my first clean shave in months. I'd get my hair cut tomorrow, somewhere out of town.

So here I was, in front of the mirror again, my hands propping me up on the dresser. It had been months since I'd seen my face, my real face. I looked tired...tired but satisfied. Since the decision to go after The Twins, this was the first chance I'd had to take stock.

It was hard to believe that Phase One wasn't just complete, it had been successful. I was never completely confident of my ability or logic. But facts were facts. I'd figured out where guns were likely to be around, done my research, gone in, and got one. Time had never really been a problem, finding the balls was.

I'd proved to myself that I could do whatever it took. I was gradually eroding the self-doubt, lack of confidence, call it what you will but I was coping. Not bad for an ageing desk jockey. More to the point, I'd done it anonymously. Now it was over, I started to actually think about what I'd done as Hamilton.

For almost a year, it had been an alien existence, one I'd thought I was ill prepared for and yet, I'd got away with it. I hoped that in shedding him, what he'd been and the things he had done, I'd be able to be human once again. My fear now, was that his might not be an easy skin to slough off. For this to work Tom Hood had needed to change but there was much of me I'd liked. Now, I wasn't so sure. I grunted at my reflection. Ignored my reservations and went to bed. I slept like a baby.

The Darkweb

Sipping coffee, I sat in my kitchen and took stock. Retrieving the gun from the drawer, I took a long, hard look at it before attempting anything. Bloody awful things really, guns. They tend not to take prisoners and I had a healthy respect for their ability to go off. It wasn't a Browning. Wearily acknowledging my ignorance, I referred to old faithful for instructions, the internet. It didn't take too long, ten minutes or so revealed that what I had was a Glock 19. I read on a while, viewed a couple of U Tube videos and once I was confident I wasn't about to shoot myself in the foot, got to work.

All Glock's have a safe action trigger to avoid accidental discharges. It took a deliberate action to make this thing fire but in the heat of the moment, if it came, I wouldn't have to worry about any safety catch. I uttered a low grunt of satisfaction and began to familiarise myself with my new best friend.

Pressing its release catch on the left-hand side of the frame, the magazine sprang down into my waiting left hand. Pulling back the top slide showed the gun to be empty, therefore safe. There are handy indicators on the back of the mag showing how many rounds are in it. Counting them, I saw I had a full mag. Fifteen 9mm rounds.

Wearing gloves now, I took an hour stripping and cleaning the body, pulling through the barrel, lightly oiling the whole and checking the action. Next, I emptied the magazine, thoroughly cleaning it inside and out and checking the rounds for damage. Finding none, I refilled the mag. Keeping my finger away from the trigger, I pulled the slide until the magazine was empty, the rounds neatly and cleanly leaving the ejection chamber, landing softly in my lap. I refilled the mag. I now had a good to go, fully operational weapon.

Though I knew I'd go through this ritual regularly, for familiarity purposes as much as forensics, for now the Glock was as clean as I could get it. With luck, there were no traces of me or anybody else to be found. From now on, I would only touch it wearing gloves. I hoped I'd done enough to prevent it being traced back to me.

I'd taken a couple of days to reorganise myself, the house, my life. Simply shaving and having my hair cut had made me feel a little like my old self and doing normal stuff like going to the supermarket felt good. TV dinners and takeaways weren't my idea of wholesome and cooking for myself again, a beer in hand, relaxed me.

My handyman, Sid, sixty-five if he was a day, also gave the place and me a sense of normalcy. I looked forward to mornings, when he'd take a break.

We'd sit in the kitchen, my guilty secret beneath our feet, and talk about life and all its rich tapestries over tea and a sandwich. He'd never been as far afield as Australia but in the past, I had, so describing where I'd been these past months didn't take too much imagination, simply saying I'd been staying with family and thrown in the occasional road trip. A shared love of crosswords developed into a duel.

I tracked more recent events via the media. The night I'd left had turned violent, as I'd hoped. Hamilton never got a mention, nor did Pete, which worked for me. I had a lot of time for Pete and had meant him no harm. I did hear that two were dead, rivals shooting it out, the radio had said. No names I knew.

Pity that, I thought. There were a couple of Benny's guys that needed putting down but at least drugs had been found and arrests made. No names given, I hoped my guys were on that list and out of circulation, at least for the time being.

The Hole and Peabody's were closed down and anyone left still standing had temporarily gone underground. All this suited me. In the chaos, a car dealer might easily have made himself scarce.

It was a shame as I'd kinda liked Fast Johnny. Ambushing him at the motorway services had been a means to an end, nothing more.

The 2 kilos of coke I'd flushed down the toilet. If Benny's claims about its purity were right, the Teenage Mutant Ninja Turtles would have been in serious party mode.

Now it was time to find the fuckers. How though? There was no one to ask, I'd have to use the system somehow. I knew they were out, but that was it. Their sentence had been an indefinite one. In other words, it would take a review before they could be considered for parole at any time, rather than a pre-determined date.

In theory, this meant they could have been locked up forever, the practice though, is somewhat different. Kids like these are sent to what are known as Secure Children's Homes. There are 10 in the UK. In a lot of cases, the kids with the longest sentences are better off than those on shorter punishment. There will be a plan. Psychological, educational, therapeutic. The end game is usually getting them through an A level education, something most kids in these places would never have attained in their previous life. These two fuckers had got degrees. Degrees for fucks sake! I'd need to find out what they'd been studying, I couldn't imagine they hadn't thought that through and elected for a field that might somehow further whatever agenda they had in mind for the future.

One thing was certain, it wouldn't have been Philosophy or Literature.

Putting them away had just made them smarter and the system was so proud of itself that it had confidently and quietly restored them to a society assured that they'd teased out the psychopath in them.

At eighteen, they should have been transferred to an adult prison. This rarely happens with any of these youngsters as it is seen as undoing all the efforts of the SCH and as these two had exceeded expectations, there was never really any chance they'd be locked up past that age. They would have known that. Mummy would have known it too. So, Eddie and Verity were out. Rehabilitated. All very laudable. But I wasn't a social worker.

The internet is a wonderful thing. Going back to when I was a kid, libraries were about the only source of information available, research had to be done in public, in silence, beneath the light of a green Bankers Lamp.

Nowadays, though, there aint much that isn't out there that you can't dig up from the comfort and relative privacy of your own home. All you need are keywords and anything electronic with the ability to connect, though naturally I had to keep an eye on how to achieve that without leaving an electronic trail.

I really didn't mind how long it took. It was just a case of getting it right. Virgo, see. Perfectionist, so they say. They'd have new identities of course, courtesy of you and me, but Christian hadn't said anything about their appearance, and I felt certain he would have, had they been radically altered. Perhaps the largesse of the public purse didn't run to plastic surgery.

There was no way they'd be logging on anywhere, legitimate, or otherwise, using their birth names. But I knew their kinks and inclinations. It was a starting point. What I needed, was The Dark Web. I hadn't the first clue how to access it, but I hoped what I needed was on it.

I powered up and typed in 'Access Darkweb' into my everyday search engine. It's astonishing to discover that anonymity is achievable. It turns out that the first rule is to find a safe country and move there. By safe I mean one that doesn't try its damnedest to spy on its citizens. Not that easy in this day and age and in my case, impractical. So, I'd have to ignore that one. Instead, it seemed, what I needed was a couple of brand-new laptops, one to establish what to do and another on which to do it, having destroyed the first one.

Next, an anonymizing operating system with secure software-based encryption. Whatever that was. I kept reading. The ultimate laptop needed to be set up to jump around random, different, open wireless networks, whether public or not and never use the same connection point.

Did you know that there are little bits of kit out there that will allow you to access the Internet from anywhere in the world without revealing your true location or IP? One of them is called a reverse GSM bridge. This little bit of genius would allow me to proxy from anywhere in the world and unless GCHQ were on my case, would never reveal my true location.

There's more, much more information than I feel the need to outline here. In short, with a bit of ready cash, some spare time, and the will to do it, being nobody is much easier to achieve than you might think. Don't use plug ins, set up burner accounts, never use credit cards. It would take a couple of weeks of research, judicial choices, careful purchases and a lot of work trawling slowly through a load of technical crap, but I reckoned when I was done, I'd be as secure as I was ever going to get. I went shopping.

I'd given Sid two weeks paid holiday, I figured that was as much time as I'd need. The cellar was massive, a prerequisite when I was house hunting, pretty much extending over the entire footprint of the house.

I'd selected a nice dry alcove close to power and water and with my expensive new tools, began building what would effectively be an underground lair.

The hardest part was cutting through the floor of the kitchen to manufacture a hidden access but with patience, in time, I had a removable floor panel and separate hidden staircase down into the cellar. Using the original staircase, I installed what furniture I needed that was too big to go through the access hatch, a desk, chair and pinboards, then built the back wall.

When complete, viewed from inside the cellar, it had all the appearance of having been there since the original building had gone up. I piled old garden furniture against it to add a further layer of disuse. I had a monitor with wireless camera feeds showing me the rest of the house and grounds and a good internet link.

Satisfied that I now had a secure workplace, I transferred the Glock underground. Time to get to the real work. With all the info I needed having been provided by the now dead laptop number one, I unpacked a fresh one but before powering it up, taped over the webcam, simple, effective, and another level of anonymity.

Settling into the chair, I switched it on. Putting in just enough garbage to get past the starter screens and into the operating system, I clicked onto the internet and downloaded a browser bundle suited to my purpose, one I'd researched and established was just the ticket. Built into the bundle was a control panel which automatically randomised my IP address. That and the GSM Bridge would keep me secure.

None of this is difficult. I ran the file and extracted it, creating an icon on my desktop. I hesitated before opening Pandora's box. It sat there, unblinking, looking for all the world like any other icon but this was going to take me into an unknown world. A place inhabited by people savvier than I'd ever be. Tom Hood had done well to get this far but deep down, despite everything I'd done these past months, I knew I was still Mister Suburbia. Drugs, guns, The Darkweb, this wasn't me. I'd had moments of doubt before and knew what I needed to kick start my resolve.

I opened the Toybox in my head, just briefly, just enough to motivate me. I thought of Ellen. I thought of The Twins. I moved my hand to the mouse and hovered over the browser icon. I had the comfort of knowing that if I got into difficulty or felt threatened in any way, all I had to do was close the browser and bin the electronics. Being prepared to start afresh was becoming a way of life. Mentally taking a deep breath, I double clicked. Bingo. I had my Darkweb browser.

The very name 'Darkweb' inspires fear but as the browser opened, not a fat lot happened. No scarlet rimmed eyes stared out at me, no steam or foul odours emanated from the laptop. It looked for all the world like any other search engine. Ever so slightly reassured, I typed them in. Edward and Verity Christian, it seemed like the logical place to start.

I'd done this before, probably a thousand times since the murder. I was more than familiar with the newspaper stories, blogs and various other websites that had sprung up all containing information and opinion. Amongst them, what you might now call my trained eye, saw a whole bunch that courtesy of the Darkweb hadn't been evident before. I'd kinda hoped this would be what I'd find.

For the first few days, I played it safe, only roaming around sites offering reports and opinion, staying away from what were obviously vigilante blogs of which there were an abundance. I printed up stuff that was new to me or of particular interest and pinned it to my board. There was some real gold in the form of a police psychologists report and transcripts of The Twins in the interview room with my policeman, Stuart Ames. Other stuff related to the various secure homes they'd been kept in, and the efforts Mummy made to have them reunited.

Lots of crap about their human rights and threats of litigation. Officialdom had crumbled under the legal onslaught, and she got her way. Eddie and Verity were, after all, very special. They'd got their degrees in record time graduating just prior to their release. I assume that as they had little else to do, they saw it as some kind of stimulus.

I'd got as much as I was going to get that was fact and as I'd trawled, I'd noted some usernames that jumped out repeatedly and when I felt confident, I tapped into them. What I was looking for, were sighting reports. There was a heap of those, I paid scant regard to any that pre-dated their release, there really are some boneheads on the web, but looked harder at those that appeared corroborated and there weren't that many, perhaps half a dozen or so.

You'd imagine that something as unique in appearance as these two would stand out but then, they would know that and have altered themselves in some way, or perhaps never appeared together in public, shopping, and the like. As individuals they would blend in and no photos of them had been published since their arrest. It got to the point where the only thing left to do was to get in the car and start checking locations around the UK.

I picked the most likely first and in descending order, got the car out and started driving.

All told I reckon I spent three months wandering, looking, watching, researching, diligently working my way through an ever-diminishing list of Darkweb rumours, and found not a single trace of them. I was running out of ideas.

Sacha

It was now August, just over a year since their release and I was on my way back from having bitten the dust on the latest 'sure' thing on the Darkweb. Lost in thought, disappointed at finding nothing from what I'd hoped was the most promising sighting so far, I'd been on autopilot. Peripherally, familiar sights began to intrude until I became fully conscious of where I was. With the satnav volume turned off, nothing had been guiding me home and I'd simply drifted back to our old hometown.

I jerked into full awareness, now alive to the possibility of bumping into Sacha. The prospect though, faded comfortably, perhaps even with a sense of disappointment, when I remembered she didn't live too close anymore, the house I'd bought her being some ten or so miles away.

I was on a roundabout on the outskirts of town, the pub sitting familiarly to my right. It was imposing enough to have its own exit lane, on impulse and lacking anything else to do, I flicked the indicator and crossing the carriageway, aimed for the car park.

Little had changed, perhaps a fresh coat of paint to the outside and hanging baskets renovated and more ambitious than I remembered. I hoped that the pub's garden still existed.

Unlike the larger, more commercial chains, this place was privately owned and run, and instead of packing the grounds with tables and benches, the owners had been content to simply make it a nice place to be with space between seating areas. Space to breathe and chat. Landscaped and planted, it was where we had spent the occasional summer weekend socialising the pup and washing away the trials of the working week. I hoped the lunches were still as good, I was hungry from the drive and though it had been nearly eight years since I'd last crossed the threshold if I came across a familiar face, well…why not? I was beginning to crave company.

Parking the Merc, I sat there for a moment or two, considering the wisdom of being here. We hadn't had a huge social circle and it had been spread far and wide. We rarely, if ever met friends here, preferring instead to gather when it had been too long since the group's last catch up, usually at each other's homes. None of them came here, it was where on a Friday evening, if I wasn't abroad on business, we had our date night.

We generally arrived separately, both coming straight from work, it made it feel more like an assignation, keeping the romance alive. I was instantly saddened by this reminder of our change in circumstances. Mentally, I shoved this to one side and allowed my curiosity to get the better of me, I got out, locked the car, and walked quietly into my past.

Above the door, a bold plate told me Jamie and Sara were still the Licensees. I twitched a bit at that but then carried on through the door. Them still being here made no difference. If asked, I was just passing through, but the reality was that I felt compelled by something. I didn't know what that something was and didn't try to analyse it, perhaps I was looking for a comfort zone, a friendly face. Time had blurred my attitude to memories, and I felt reasonably confident I could deal with them if, or more likely, when they occurred.

Inside it was pretty much the way I'd remembered it. Clean, cared for and homely. Most of the furniture had changed but the layout of the interior kinda dictated the seating plan and much of that remained. Including our corner. A small, circular bar table flanked by two high backed chairs and framed by a picture window offering daylight and a view.

My eyes pricked, then moistened. From time to time, that table had been occupied when we'd arrived for date night. It had amused me how Sacha couldn't settle until it had been vacated. Grabbing her bag and drink, she'd quickly scuttle across the room and grab it like a trophy. Then, and only then, could our evening begin.

Overcoming my brief, gloomy moment, I pushed back the doldrums and smiled at the memory of it.

Behind the bar, another; and given the time lapse and staff wastage nature of the trade, somewhat surprising echo of the past, bustled. She glanced over once to acknowledge a new presence then did a double take.

"It's you!"

"So it is." I replied, offering a slight smile. "How many now Em?"

Her eyes crinkled and a wide smile replaced her surprise. "Oh, just the two still. I reckon I'm done."

When we'd first moved into the area, Emma had been approaching her twenties and single. During our patronage, marriage and two kids had come her way but through it all she'd kept working. I guess the pub was as much a part of her life as the family she'd acquired over the years.

I ordered a pint and there was silence as it was poured. Placing it on the bar, as kindly as she could, Emma broached the subject we both knew was uppermost. This was the first time I'd been back to the pub since the murder, the Press putting an end to our date nights.

"We were all so…I'm sorry, but it was just…"

I leaned on the bar and picked up my drink. "It's ok, Em. We meant to thank you for the flowers, but some good intentions got lost in the mess. For the record, we really appreciated them."

The pub had sent a wreath to Ellen's funeral, it wasn't store bought but handmade and had come from their own garden, it was all the more meaningful for it.

"It's done, Em. Eight years now. I'm ok, honest."

"I know but still…we, I'm sorry." She was choked and I wasn't far away. To break the mood, she trotted off and made herself busy behind the bar.

Standing there, in this most familiar of places, I couldn't resist the urge to turn and look at our corner. The place was relatively empty, I could have sat anywhere I guess, but I couldn't sit somewhere else looking at it, imagining handbags and drinks being swiftly ferried over nor did I want anyone else to sit there, changing the memory. So, taking my pint in hand, I wandered over and sat down. It might not have been the same chair, but it was in the same place. The view unchanged except for Sacha's absence.

Word had clearly got out that I'd turned up. Sara came from behind the bar clutching a small drink.

Despite running a pub, Sara generally abstained, until she discovered a curious toffee vodka when on a cruise holiday. It was the only tipple she enjoyed but I'd never seen her with one in her hand before. She sat down, thoughtfully, not where Sacha would have been.

"Hello stranger. Alright, are you?" Though this was a small, former mining town in Leicestershire, Sara was Welsh and her lilting accent apparent. We'd liked coming here and Sara was part of why.

"Fair to middling." I acknowledged.

It's true to say I was enjoying the familiarity of this link to the past. Twin hunting was a solitary occupation and since The Hole, with the exception of Sid, my gardener, and the occasional conversation when fuelling the Merc, I'd had little in the way of human contact.

"Jamie ok?" I asked, struggling for small talk.

"He's in the kitchen, being creative."

The conversation stuttered, awkwardly. Nature abhors a vacuum and despite the usual background activity in the pub, I felt I was in one. I glanced around for inspiration.

"Her bottle is still there." I nodded at the back of the bar.

Sacha was and possibly still is, a white spirit girl. Date nights weren't just for flirting with each other. Sacha had expressed an interest in craft gins and vodkas and Sara, good as gold, had furnished a variety of interesting and unusual concoctions, most of which went untouched by the regular clientele. Sacha had eventually declared an exotic craft gin to be her favourite of these. There was a half empty bottle of it on a shelf behind the bar.

"Wrong." Sara countered. "I have to source that stuff about once a month. That's not the same bottle."

"Sara," I said, leaning forward, "There is no way your regulars would touch that stuff, not being cruel or typecasting anyone, but it's a tad exotic and Sacha a bit possessive. Unless your customer base has gravitated away from its roots...that would have to be the same bottle."

Mimicking my conspiratorial pose, Sara leaned towards me and cocked her head. "It hasn't, and it isn't."

Leaning back, Sara took a genteel sip from her vodka, then casually dropped the bomb.

"Sacha still comes here. Every Friday night and sometimes at the weekends." She nodded to the chair on my left.

"She sits there, I sit here, she's got me breaking my own rules." Sara raised the glass in her hand as evidence.

I sat back, perhaps a little abruptly. The house I'd bought her was at least ten miles away and a fair old way to come for a drink, even if it was for a bizarre gin. I wasn't going to let on that I knew she'd moved but felt reasonably assured I could ask the question without appearing too interested or aware.

"I thought she'd moved?"

Sara smiled. "Oh, that place. You know I like to keep a few quid spare, just in case of emergencies? Well, when she told me about this mystery house, me and Jamie went with her to have a look at it. Lovely. Really lovely. We're renting it out at the mo. We're going to retire there...if we ever bloody retire."

Something else that hadn't crossed my mind. That Sacha might not want the house.

"You bought it?"

"Lock, stock and barrel." Sara declared. "A bargain too. Fair but no messing, which was how she wanted it."

"She's still down the road?" My surprise was evident and complete. Our old house was a ten-minute walk away, eight if you had the dog.

"That's right. Never moved."

This was way too close for comfort, and I felt oddly flustered. I hadn't really counted but it had been maybe six years since the divorce and as I hadn't asked the Jedi for anything but protection for her, they'd had no reason or brief to offer anything but that. They didn't call me, I called them, that was the arrangement.

"It's been nice, Sara." I put down my half-finished pint and made ready to leave.

"Not so fast, young man." Jesus, I was anything but that. Not much of the young man left in me but that was Sara's way.

"She's outside. In the garden with the dog. You'd best take yourself out there."

That wasn't part of the plan. I accepted that something had brought me here and until now, it had been a pleasant diversion, but the last feelings I'd had towards Sacha, had been inadequacy and sadness and I'd journeyed too far in myself to go down that road again. My heart said go outside. My head said run. In-between though, a sense of curiosity elbowed its way in. Perhaps I could. Maybe even should. It was Sara that toppled the scales.

"Tom, Sacha and me…we talk."

She gave me a knowing look. "Go into the garden. I've planted lilies, you'll love it. Take your drink. I'll keep an eye out if it looks like running dry."

Sacha must have asked for this, Sara wouldn't have pushed me if she hadn't, the sisterhood at work. It seemed I had little choice and wondered whether I'd have exercised it if I had. I picked up my unfinished pint and followed her through the bar. Sara pushed the outer door open and nodded.

"Out you go." I went.

Being sunny, most benches were occupied. Families mainly, not what I was looking for. Then I saw her, a solitary figure with a small, dark dog by her feet. Pooh. It was the first real word that had been recognisable amongst Ellen's baby babble. She'd been about nine months old when we'd bought the dog on the principle, right or wrong, that every child should have one. It had been my idea on the basis that I remembered few of my toys but every pet that had belonged to my family.

House training consisted of shouting, 'Poo!' whenever the pup had squatted and shooing him out into the garden. Ellen had picked it up and for a week or so it was all she would say, so the name changed from Biscuit, to Pooh, we added the 'H' mentally, all the quicker to forget any connotations the word without it implied. My legs feeling suddenly weak, somehow carried me over. She looked up.

"Hey you." Clearly unsurprised, having been told I was here, the words said simply, a brief smile flitting over her face.

Pooh stirred, looked at me and yawned, collapsing back onto the grass. *No recognition there, then.* Sacha's mid-western drawl had softened over the last six years or so but still gave me goosebumps.

"Hi." Was as good as I could give, my throat tightening. Sacha gestured to the other side of the bench, so I sat.

She had always been the most exotic creature in my world and looking at her now, nothing had changed. She looked simply stunning. Her hair was different, auburn still but now bobbed and featuring carefully engineered highlights. It suited her. No makeup, she didn't need it and rarely wore it and there were perhaps a few lines on her face that hadn't been there, but Sacha and her essence, still hit me. She wore a light jacket against the breeze, black leggings, and trainers…walking clothes. If she'd gained weight, I couldn't tell. Being this close to her, after all this time, set me trembling. I clasped my hands together in an attempt to quell it.

"You look well. Been working out? And no limp?"

"I'm good, thanks. The doctors sorted out the limp."

Pumping weights was out of character for the old Tom Hood, so I made no response on that front. This was the fittest I'd been since I'd let myself go after the event. I became aware I was being studied.

She was looking directly at me, into me.

"There's something else about you that's different." I sat there, uncomfortable under the microscope.

"Should I ask or are you going to tell me?"

No preamble, direct and occasionally discomfiting, she had a knack of phrasing a question that left you no option other than to respond. I had little to offer though. I hadn't anticipated being here and certainly hadn't expected to bump into Sacha. Sid aside, who knew nothing of the old Tom Hood, I hadn't had to explain myself to anyone since the meeting with Christian. I'd had limited contact with humanity and as no cover story had been needed…I didn't have one. I knew I'd changed since my last physical contact with Sacha but hadn't considered that there might be outward evidence of it. Whatever it was, Sacha had clocked it.

"Doing much?" She asked. My silence had perhaps answered her question for her.

She must have known I wasn't with the airline anymore, but it seemed like a casual query. My problem remained. I wasn't used to being quizzed and had nothing prepared. Millionaire Twin hunter would not be an appropriate answer.

"A bit of freelance consultation, it pays the bills." Vague, I know, but it was the best I had.

"Tom, I saw the car…and those clothes you're wearing…I know designer when I see it." She leaned forwards.

"What," she said, "are you really doing?" She didn't wait for my answer, she was on a roll. I'd had these kinds of conversations with Sacha before. They were one sided back then and this one was turning out to be no different.

"Someone... anonymous, bought me an expensive house and car. Out of the blue I had a phone call from a solicitor. Good news, something to my advantage etc... could I come to his office? Perhaps morning appointments work better for most of his clients but mine was post lunch…which he'd had at the pub. Most of it, apparently liquid. Do you know anything about that?"

She paused. She knew I was on the back foot but instead of pressing her advantage home, she softened, leaning back. "But that's by the by. I have a real question; one you can answer."

I was struggling a bit. Roleplay I can do, outright lying though, wasn't my strong point. She'd know. Oddly though, her next words let me off the hook a little.

"How are you? I mean really, how are you?"

"In what sense?" I was playing for time, trying to get my act together.

She shuffled impatiently, a clear sign that this wasn't going to be a comfortable conversation.

"Ok," she said. "I'm going to tell you a story. When I'm done, I want to know how you are and hopefully then you'll understand the question and I'll eventually get my answer."

Her tone changed from inquisitive to one of regret.

"It seems like a lifetime ago now, but I once had a man in my life. A man, simple in his own way but in saying that I don't mean dim. Before him, there had, of course, been others. I'd even had proposals of marriage. Tempting offers but never enough. I needed someone I could depend on. I mean utterly depend on. So, I waited until eventually he came. That man was you, Tom." There was an intensity in her voice, but it was more apparent in her expression, a deep need to convey a message.

"My life was complete. Fulfilled even, made more so by our Ellen. What happened next, to Ellen and how it changed you, left me with nothing. It shouldn't have been that way. You had an indefinable something that gave me hope, hope that you were the one I'd waited for, someone I truly believed I could depend on…and you, you let me down."

I was about to interrupt but was stopped by a raised hand.

"Hush your mouth, Tom Hood. This is my story, and you have to hear it. Maybe I should have done this at the time but if I'm going to be honest with you, I must be honest with myself. Perhaps if I'd been more open, we'd still be married, but I wasn't. I don't know how much of what happened to us was my fault and if I let you down in any way, any way at all, I'm truly sorry. But it was you that shocked me, Tom. You crumbled. The one time we really needed each other you just broke apart and left me standing there, feeling alone. One of the reasons why I fell in love with you in the first place is your over developed sense of responsibility, a real sense of the difference between right and wrong but your sensitivity, that brain of yours, broke you". She paused, her tone changing from what might have been condemnation to one of regret.

"You are a fixer, Tom. Someone who when presented with a problem, finds joy in providing a solution but when that problem is an emotional one rather than practical one, where perhaps the simple answer is just to offer support, you couldn't do it. Maybe you don't have the words. I don't know. But when you found yourself helpless to change anything that had happened, when there was nothing practical, hands on, that you could apply yourself to, you ran. Mentally and physically, the one thing, the one person I truly felt I could rely on had simply melted away, turned inwards, if you like. That wasn't the man I needed, Tom. It wasn't the man Ellen needed so, until that man resurfaced, I cut him loose. Do you remember how easy it was for you to leave? How easy I made it for you?"

She let the question hang between us as I thought back. There had never been arguments, no smashing of crockery or blazing rows. Just a shift in mood and trust, a dropping off from a sense of belonging, of togetherness. I looked across at her. I got the feeling that her point was about to be made as I watched her eyes change. It was subtle. An almost imperceptible adjustment in colour, from blue to grey.

"So, Tom. How are you? Are you the man I thought you were or are you still feeling sorry for yourself?"

Was this the point where I was supposed to tell her everything? When I'd lost Sacha's respect, I'd kinda known that we were in the end game and looking back, perhaps that had been the point where my decline had been complete. We'd been two people who knew that without having to measure it, had total faith in each other. We were friends. It was as fulfilling as it could get, for us at least.

Part of me imagined that by running my mouth off at how I'd become an avenging angel might somehow bring that back. But how could I? How do you begin a conversation like that? Was she looking to see if I'd matured emotionally? That I'd somehow become more able to understand what she needed to see us both through the turmoil of Ellen's murder?

I had no answer to that. My way of dealing with it, of picking myself up from the floor, of scouring events, was reprisal. I hadn't thought about the kind of epilogue Sacha was seeking. Did she want the twins' dead? If I told her, would I come away with her respect as the man she remembered, or would I be condemned as a dreamer fantasising about retribution? I shouldn't have come here.

Until now, I'd had purpose and a clear idea of how it would end.

But sitting here, opposite someone I'd never stopped aching for, I felt the need to regain some pride and sense of honour, to make her feel that I was worthwhile, strong, brave, and solid. Someone dependable. Her fixer, she'd said.

There was also the sure and absolute knowledge that I loved her. I missed her. I craved my place beside her and knew that the truth was the only route that I could follow and be believed, trying to feed her anything else would lack credibility and she would simply see through the lies without understanding their purpose. That could only end with her contempt.

I couldn't leave without grasping at the possibility that there might be a way back for us and right now, with what she knew or remembered, that would never happen. Only a fresh narrative could undermine old impressions. Mentally weighing up the repercussions of confessing, I was fairly certain that if I told her everything, she wouldn't involve the Police, the worst-case scenario was that she would walk away, so I had nothing to lose and the possibility, however remote, that I had everything to gain.

So, I told her. All of it. Christian, the money, The Hole in the Wall. The gun and the hunt.

She listened, impassive, occasionally thoughtful, impatient only when I lost my train of thought and had to wend my way back to it, via chronology or stark memories. Only her eyes expressed surprise but to my relief, no consternation or concern. The conversation, albeit one sided, was occasionally interrupted as Sara spotted the need for refreshments and duly delivered.

My tale took the rest of the afternoon and evening began to fall. When I was done, I sat quietly, nursing my latest pint, which had gone flat. I wasn't a great conversationalist and the last couple of hours had emptied my word bank. I was now a waiting man. Waiting to be judged, waiting to see how my admission would be received.

"Thank You." Two simple words expressed in a way that said it all. Everything about her had softened. Even the failing light had mellowed the edges of what, for me, had been a petrifying experience.

"Your solicitor was pissed, Tom. I knew you'd bought the house and car. He never said as much but I knew it had to be you. I was mystified by where the money had come from, I thought maybe you'd won the lottery or something."

She leaned towards me over the bench and laid a hand on mine.

"What you're doing…mad and extreme as it seems sitting here listening to it…it's the right thing. I can't justify it or at least, in another life I couldn't, but in my heart, I feel that some things, right or wrong, need to be done.' She paused briefly, wavering.

"I've never mentioned this before, and before I do, I'm telling you that this isn't a criticism, that I understand…really do understand…why you didn't watch the video shown in court."

She waited for a reaction from me, I had nothing to offer but a sense of shame. Sacha shouldn't have had to go through that alone but if I had a chance to sit through it with her now, I still wouldn't be able to do it. I don't have a coping mechanism for it. She continued.

"But I did. I saw it all. I didn't want to, I shouldn't have had to, but I sat through it."

She paused again, raw emotion halting the flow of words, her eyes downcast.

"It was abominable, vile...the memory of it will never, ever leave me." Her head came up and she looked me straight in the eye, her expression grim.

"I 'aint gonna lie to you. I'd considered doing something drastic myself but couldn't see how. Before Ellen, before we actually needed justice, I suppose I never really thought too hard about how the system works. But now, when I think about them, what they did and how they're getting on with their lives, getting away with it…I don't think I've ever felt more hate towards anyone or anything." Her eyes misted and her voice almost broke with emotion.

"They're free and clear, Tom. It's wrong. Just fucking wrong."

Sacha rarely swore, using profanity for emphasis, not punctuation. Even with a few drinks inside me, I was taken aback. Her eyes flashed fiercely, ablaze at the implied injustice of her last sentence. It was a look I hadn't seen before and in my new identity as avenger, I liked it. I liked it very much. I wondered though, how the world might look on another day, after we'd both sobered up and considered what had happened here today.

It was obvious I wasn't driving anywhere. At the back of my mind, the idea surfaced that Sara, in providing a steady flow of drinks had undertaken some kind of social experiment.

A taxi would be stupidly expensive, and I'd have to come back in the morning for the car, it didn't matter that I had the money to pay for it, it was a waste, something Sacha and I abhorred.

Saying goodnight to Sara was surreal, following Sacha's surprise suggestion to crash for the night at 'her' place, we took a trip back in time as with Pooh leading, we walked unsteadily from the pub to the house. Even with the dog, keen to get home, it was slow going but eventually, we turned the corner and I saw our old home. There was a Porsche parked outside.

"I kept the car." Sacha said with a smile. "I'm not completely stupid."

Inside, the house was much as I remembered it. Apart from new carpets, little had changed. My DIY handiwork appeared to have stood the test of time, shelving and the like still intact. The main difference was the decoration on the staircase and first floor landing. Sacha had selected old photographs and had them blown up into canvasses. From the bottom of the stairs, winding up them and around the landing all the way to the upstairs bathroom was our life writ large. Ellen much in evidence. It took an effort of will to drag my eyes away. I hadn't been able to look at our daughter since a couple of days after she'd died.

"Deliberate." She said. "Every morning and every night, these are the first and last things I see. It helps."

"I'll take the sofa."

"Damn right you will. This conversation isn't over. I want the Twins dead."

She disappeared upstairs, Pooh trailing her. In the dark, alone, I wondered what I'd begun.

I was woken by a stiff back and Pooh's wet nose sniffing my hand. Abruptly, I was reminded where I was. I heard noises coming from the kitchen along with the aroma of fresh coffee. Sacha came through into the lounge, carrying two mugs of it. She was wrapped in my old bathrobe. A small detail but it was something we'd wrestled over in the past. I knew for a fact she had several fluffy, girly one's but way back, it had always been a race between us to grab my ratty, old grey one. If I'd lost, early mornings had me looking and feeling faintly ridiculous in one of hers. She'd always said mine made her feel cosy. It was a poignant reminder.

"Morning."

It came out as more of a grunt, not what I'd intended. Yesterday had me hoping that there just might be enough embers to spark a reconciliation, something I hadn't thought possible before. But Sacha's reaction to me, to my story, had fired up a new hope.

Twin hunting was no longer enough for me. When that was done, I wanted our life back. But for the time being at least, I thought it wise to leave those kinds of ideas on the back burner. Life was complicated enough without adding dreaming to the mix.

"Morning." She responded brightly, handing me the coffee then taking a seat on the other sofa.

"What next?" She asked.

I wasn't in my best thinking mode as I struggled to sit upright while juggling my coffee and keeping a hold on the quilt I'd slept under. The dog wasn't helping, sitting right where I needed to plant my feet. Gaining the vertical at last, I ran my free hand through my hair, trying to establish some degree of a civilised appearance. The coffee tasted good and gave me a chance to think of a response. Sacha sat quite still, alert and waiting.

"I'm not sure you should get involved. It would complicate things."

"Really?" I knew that tone. It said, *I don't think so.*

She shuffled on the sofa, as if gaining purchase before going on the assault. I knew she wanted the same as me and from her reaction and attitude yesterday, perhaps wasn't fussy about how it was done. But I treasured this girl, this woman. I always had. Placing her in harm's way or risking her freedom had left me confused and unable to adapt my thinking. Until yesterday, I had clarity and a single-minded pursuit that hadn't cared much about the consequences to me. Now I had someone else to consider.

"Think about it, Sacha. This isn't the Wild West, the law of the gun with little chance of prosecution. We're talking about murder here. This isn't a decision about which curtains we should have, sofa to buy or where to go on holiday. It's going to change your life. Perhaps even put you in jail."

"Change my life?" That tone again. "Change my life?!"

The repetition had gone up an octave and I could see and hear pain. Her voice trembled as she teetered on the edge of tears. "Please don't think, not even for a minute, that you can't involve me." There was emphasis on the *can't*.

She collected herself, quietly clenching her fists, knuckles whitening as she continued.

"There was a time when my world was complete, Tom. I truly believed, right down to the depths of my soul, the core of me, that we were swans. You and me, together for life, elegantly cruising along, growing old side by side, never missing a beat. When Ellen arrived, well, there was a gloss to everything and so much to look forward to. Loving that child added a new dimension to me, an inexplicable other place that she created, and I lived in alongside of her. There was more colour there, heightened senses, new horizons". She shuffled in her chair.

"I'm going to try to explain to you where that place came from and maybe then you'll understand the vacuum left behind now that place is empty. How colourless, barren, and flat it is. How empty I am." She paused, relaxed, and softly remembered.

"When I found out I was pregnant, well, you know how exciting and new that was but really, it was only the beginning. I started to read, wanted to know what was happening inside me. Then, as I felt it happening, felt myself swell, saw myself changing shape, I began to understand how real and unique it was. Reading about how she was developing was only a fraction of my understanding it. My blood was her blood, her fingernails were mine, I could look into her eyes and see the light in them, knew when her eyelashes began to grow, framing the china blue I knew they'd be.

Then, when she began to move inside me, felt a rush. When she wriggled to get comfortable, I felt more than just happy, this little human had everything she needed, and it was me that was giving it. I knew exactly how she would look long before she left my body and was placed in my arms. At that point, from that point, if I'd had to die for her, I'd have been sad at not seeing her through life but would gladly have done it while softly whispering, *I love you*." She choked then, struggling with the next words.

"Then, I watched as she was used, mutilated, tortured and then…killed. All as part of some sick game. Til then, I guess I was feeling pretty much the way you did. Sad, desolated, lost. But watching that video...cold fury, a deep, teeth grinding, bone crunching, blood chilling fury. No other way to describe it. Then, when that bitch and her law took away her identity, her soul and turned her into just the reason those two vile animals were stood in the dock. Knowing that, having her stripped from me and watching every punch, kick and burn it took to end her, enjoying themselves while they did it, do you honestly think I've had any kind of life? Any kind of purpose? That little girl, *our* little girl was bound to my soul, and since she's been gone...it's been limbo, Tom. Limbo. Just going through the motions, trying to forget because there was no other choice. No way to strike back. To have to just suck it up.

What I have is no kind of life, simply breathing doesn't count. You aren't the only one who needs more than we've been palmed off with. I said it last night and I'll say it again now, in the clear light of day without a drink inside me. I want them dead."

There was malevolence in that last sentence, malevolence, and determination. I understood that because it was in me. My emotional freefall and crash to earth had been perhaps more spectacular and destructive than Sacha's but sitting opposite her now, finally acknowledging what six years ago I'd been unable to see through my own veil of misery, it was clear she'd hit the deck just as hard as I had and remembering that she'd suffered through identifying Ellen's body alone. Then, during the court case, having to watch the video, again, alone because I simply couldn't bring myself to sit through it, I had to acknowledge that despite appearances, she was probably as damaged as I was, maybe even more so, she just hid it better.

Christian had handed me a lifeline, giving me the means to at least believe in the possibility of payback had dragged me out of the gutter, patched me up and brought me this far. I couldn't be certain of Sacha's emotional state but then mine wasn't exactly rock steady. Knowing how empowered I'd become since setting out, I knew I couldn't deny that sense of worth to the one person left on this planet that I actually cared about.

If she'd been a bloke as emotionally involved and motivated as me, would I let her in? the answer would be a resounding Yes.

"It's no good asking you if you know what you're getting into, even I don't know what might need to be done."

"I don't care. I stopped caring after Ellen died. I stopped caring about you, me, us, everything that mattered to me. Don't shut me out, Tom. Please. I need to be involved. I have to do something to blank those awful memories. That means they must pay. Right or wrong, there's a balance that needs resetting even if it's only in my head. I need to look at them and see the same things I saw in Ellen's eyes just before she died. Please, Tom. I can't live knowing they're taking the piss, enjoying, remembering what they did. Their memories can't be allowed to exist."

That was the nub of it. In a few words, she had just expressed exactly what it was that motivated me. The fancy legal crap that had restored The Twins to society said nothing of the legacy of their deeds, gave nothing to the dead or those that loved them. A sense of violation, polluted lives and grief are the reality of those left behind. I would have been driven mad had I not been given the lifeline of revenge, of a good, old-fashioned eye for an eye.

I had to give her the same thing I needed. Something tangible that said, 'Fuck you', to the system and pay back the vile little shits that had completely fucked up our lives and ended a precious one.

But I was frightened by the idea. It would be us bucking convention with no knowing how it would end. I'd resigned myself to the idea that I might get caught but decided that it didn't matter. But involving Sacha?

She was calm now, her business head back on. "I already have an idea. How to find them, something you might not have thought about."

I couldn't imagine what that might be. I'd covered all the bases and thought about little else for months. There was no way she had an idea I hadn't already considered and discounted or tried so I sat, waiting, ready to give her the put down. "How so?"

"Are you going to let me get involved?"

I didn't think I had a choice, Sacha knowing, but left out…there were any number of things that she might inadvertently do to jeopardise the end result. Also, I'd hit a wall, the Darkweb had given me insight and information, but nothing that got me where I needed to go. If she thought she had a way over that wall, I'd listen.

The decision to let her in was relatively simple but I had to limit her involvement and therefore, culpability.

"Ideas only, research, no dirty work. Ok?"

"It'll do for a start." She paused, serving notice that my limits on her involvement were negotiable.

"I've been thinking on part of what you said last night. How long have you been following stuff found on the Dark Web?"

"Just over three months."

"Why?" She said. "When there is a far simpler solution, one that doesn't involve loonies, sexy equipment, or risk you being found out? You've over thought this, Tom."

This would have to be good to get me to admit to a schoolboy error. I waited, sceptical and ready to reply with something cutting. I'd been at this for a while now and was a self-taught expert.

"Where," she paused for effect, "is the one place…who is the one person that no matter what, at some point, most likely Christmas and Birthdays, they are sure to meet up with?"

I sat, confused. A state of mind that lasted only milliseconds, then it dawned on me. She saw the realisation on my face.

"For months, you've been tracking down sightings, most likely imagined by nutters, when all you had to do was keep an eye on Mummy."

Mrs. Christian. She was the key and Sacha had cleared away all the clutter and got to a realistic starting point straight off the bat. I could see a sense of triumph in her expression, that despite all my manoeuvrings and attention to detail, I'd been too focussed to see something which now that she'd said it, should have been blindingly obvious from the beginning.

Jesus. Clearly, two heads are better than one. Add to the mix the female psyche and a different thought process, then perhaps together, we could get this thing some momentum.

"Teamwork." I said, admitting defeat perhaps ungraciously.

I felt disappointed in myself at not having even considered Mummy to be the answer but that was set aside by the notion of having a sounding board, a confidante, an alternative viewpoint that might at last help me achieve what I'd set out to do.

"Ok. The bitch is high profile, busy and newsworthy. My guess is that it will be gaps in her diary, particularly, as you said, around Christmas and birthdays that we need to concentrate on. Our problem now is accessing that diary."

"No, it isn't. But you're halfway there. We don't need her diary. We know the date of their birthday, October, we can find out hers and Christmas is well set into the calendar. We focus on those three events. It doesn't matter if one or two are no shows, we only need to find them once, then we've got them."

Yet again, she was right. The Twin's birthday was due in eight weeks, there might be time to get ourselves in place. If not, Christmas was four months away. If Mummy's birthday fell in between, good. Failing that, we'd have to be patient. It would also give us time to make some decisions.

"Let's get dressed, pick up your car and go for breakfast. We have some domestic arrangements to sort out."

"What do you mean?"

"Tom, we're going to be seen together, people will talk, especially as it's us. Sooner or later, we're going to have to say something."

She was right, of course. Our 'reunion' would be newsworthy whether we liked it or not. "What do you propose?"

"I haven't really thought it through. Things are happening quite quickly. Perhaps our stand ought to be that we're attempting a reconciliation."

"Are we?" It was a stupid but irresistible question.

She looked at me and while not exactly melting, she didn't say no. She focussed instead on the mug in her hands.

"Tom, we didn't divorce because I stopped loving you. My head doesn't work like that. We divorced because I couldn't bear to look at what you'd become, and I had to get out before I started despising you."

Ouch. That hurt, just the word, despise, stung. She saw my bruised expression and offered me a balm.

"I'm not saying I was brilliant to be around either, but something had to give." She leaned forward.

"Looking at you now, listening to you…I'll not deny that I see something of the old you and that's good, Tom, really good. But it's too soon to say how much of me is left. So, I'll say this, it's not a closed door, Tom. What we were was so very important and I hope we find a way back. If settling this score does that, then I'll be content and can rest and maybe remember what it was to be part of something that mattered. If we do this together, as unpleasant as it might get, it doesn't have to be bleak or grim. Enjoying it would be wrong but doing it together, working together, might fix more than we imagine. Does that make sense?"

It did. It meant that this wasn't about me or what I wanted any more. I won't pretend to understand the kind of bond that grows between a mother and daughter, but the realisation hit me that Sacha had been hurt much more than I had. Her child wrenched away and then her husband self-destructing, she, more than anyone…more than me, was entitled to her moment. If I could, I would see that she got it. That was now my function. To set things right. I mentally adjusted my priorities.

"Can I see your place?"

"Place?"

"Tom, you must live somewhere. I'm curious is all."

I'd gripped myself and with a new assurance, moved forward, comfortable in my role.

"Ready when you are."

"Ok. Dress, pick up car, house." She abbreviated.

Standing, she left the room, and I heard her pottering around upstairs. As I retrieved yesterday's clothes and dressed, my mind was in overdrive. As it whirred through the thoughts and emotions crowding it, the impression I was left with was that I had a job to do. I could fix something. I felt more human than I had in years.

I could see her in my rear-view mirror. Sacha was a faster driver than I was and clearly impatient to see the house, the Porsche large behind me. Through the gates and up the driveway she pulled in alongside me. We went in.

"Very nice, Tom Hood. You seem to be doing well for yourself."

Sid wasn't in evidence, so I showed her around and then unearthed the war room. All my research. She wanted to see the gun. I opened the drawer but before I could retrieve it. Sacha reached in and picked it up.

"Careful," I warned, reaching to recover it but she turned sideways, blocking me. "It's loaded."

She looked at me with good-humoured disdain, slipped out the magazine, made the gun safe then deftly, with sure movements, stripped and reassembled it. I thought better of referring to my U Tube education, even though mentally I had to acknowledge a degree of envy with how at ease she seemed with a gun in her hand.

"You never thought to mention this before?"

"Montana girl, honey."

It had been a while since I'd had that endearment aimed at me and my stomach did a little flip.

"It 'aint the kind of topic that comes up in conversation over fondue. I've been handling guns since I was a kid. Daddy made sure I knew how to use one. First on a shooting range with these peashooters then hunting with rifles."

"I suppose you can ride too?"

"With or without a saddle. I also know how to skin a couple of rats." She said meaningfully, putting the Glock back in the drawer.

It crossed my mind that the gun might be another bathrobe tussle. Sacha was edging her way into the meat of my scheme and having been solo for so long, it felt uncomfortable. I wasn't used to sharing.

"You went to a lot of trouble for that, Tom. Are you sure you can use it?"

I was. But now there was uncertainty as to which of us was best qualified. Without waiting for a reply, she followed that question up with another.

"How was it, the whole experience?"

"You're asking about The Hole?" She nodded.

I paused briefly, trying to sum up all the thought processes, physical actions, and downright criminal activities I'd put myself through.

"Weird. Good though. I found out a whole lot of things about myself that I wasn't aware I could do."

"Cocaine?"

I detected a hint of disapproval.

"A means to an end. Nothing more. It's done now."

"Any girls?" She let the question hang briefly then, as my mouth opened to reply, continued, "I think we should base ourselves at my house. If we can, we need to keep this place secret. Being remote, as it is, it's easy to spot a tail if we pick one up."

It struck me as remarkable how easily Sacha had slipped into clandestine mode. Thinking ahead and avoiding detection being part of it.

"My thoughts exactly." I said, establishing that I did actually possess a brain. "It's why I bought it."

"On that subject, how much money do you have left?"

I thought briefly, the sums involved were huge and not dwelling on the future, I hadn't really felt the need to keep track, so I made a semi educated guess. "Probably about six million, give or take. You know interest rates are low but some of my spending has been replaced by interest on the capital. I reckon I've spent about a million so far, but that's mostly houses, and cars so hasn't been frittered away. Does it matter?"

"It might."

Her words and the way she said them appeared to express an expectation of assuming control. I'd expended a huge amount of time and effort and taken not a little risk in my pursuit. It seemed to me that in less than 24 hours, Sacha had somehow managed to gain some ascendancy; was assuming a role that I wasn't yet prepared to relinquish. I'd either have to let it slide, avoid a confrontation I didn't want, or stamp my foot. On the other hand, I liked having her near me and didn't want to appear petulant.

Conflicting emotions left me confused. I knew I needed to say something but wasn't sure what it would be until it came out of my mouth. I desperately wanted it to make sense. Thinking on the hoof, I took her gently by the shoulders and eased her down into the chair. Slightly taken aback, she didn't resist.

"Sacha, please. I know how much you want to be a part of this. I'm starting to realise that you have every reason to be more motivated than me and I'm ashamed of how selfish and introverted I was. But…this has been my life for more than a year. I've studied, researched, planned, taken myself to places I hadn't thought existed and done things I wish I hadn't had to do." I paused, softened my tone which had developed an edge I didn't like.

"You must know how I feel about you and I'm guessing that you also know that if you had a mind to, you could twist me around your little finger and get exactly what you want, when you want it. But I'm asking you to take a step back. To stop thinking about what you want and think instead how best to achieve it. Be easy on me. Help me. Work with me. This is not a competition. We have to be clinical, not emotional, not think just of the end game, but of how to get in and out of it in one piece." I knelt beside her, our eyes at the same level.

"You can help, you already have. But it frightens me to involve you. I don't want anything happening to you. It would mean that instead of getting something back, I'd have lost everything that ever meant anything to me."

Her eyes lost some of the huffiness I'd seen as I'd been speaking. On a roll, I continued.

"The situation as I see it is a simple one. Had The Twins not come into our lives, we would still have one. We would still have Ellen. But they did. To get back to living, whether together or apart, they have to be dealt with." I didn't like the words but said them anyway. "They have to die, but I will not lose you trying to do it."

"Coffee?" She said, brightly.

I didn't know whether that meant she understood what I'd said or was simply trying to defuse what had at least for me, become a fraught situation. I nodded and we climbed back up into the kitchen. Knowing there'd be questions and some discussion, I took my file case up with me. I heard the kettle going on as I adjusted the flooring until I was content the war room access was invisible. We sat quietly over our coffee as Sacha thought, and I let her do it. Presently, she looked up.

"I'm with you, Tom." I figured she hadn't finished and waited.

"I'll admit you have a point. Perhaps I was getting a bit ahead of myself. But…and I know this is the wrong word to use, I'm excited by this. Not just what you're doing but the fact that you're actually doing it." She hesitated momentarily.

"I did come to the hospital you know. I poked my head around the door, you were asleep, so I left. If I'm honest, I didn't really recognise the person in that bed and remembering him, I wasn't sure who or what had turned up yesterday. But I see you now, Tom…I see you."

The hospital visit was an eye opener but irrelevant now. We both knew where we stood, and both wanted the same thing. I sensed that there would be no more jockeying or that it would at least be minimised.

Sacha stood and nursing her cup, walked to the kitchen window.

'It's beautiful here, Tom.' I joined her and we stood side by side, not touching, looking out over the grounds.

Having other priorities, I hadn't really considered the aspect of the place when I'd bought it. But she was right. The back of the house had an uninterrupted view of lawns which lead to meadows with a thick bank of trees off into the distance. As far as the eye could see, there was nothing but nature and all of it came with the house. Deer roamed occasionally, rabbits grazed frequently, and I recalled that from time to time, buzzards cruised overhead. Way back, I'd have killed for a view like this. There was a certain irony to the fact that I only owned it now, in order to do just that. Sacha broke the silence, gently touching my arm.

"You won't have to worry about me, Tom. I know you will but try not to let it affect what we do. I can take care of myself and as much as a girl appreciates a knight in shining armour, this lady has some sharp edges of her own."

We regained the breakfast bar and got down to business.

"What do we know so far about The Twins?"

I didn't have a fat lot to add but uncertain how much Sacha knew; I trotted out what I had.

"We know they got out last October. We know they have new identities. While they were inside, they got degrees. She in Psychology, him in I.T. I have no idea why they opted for those specific subjects, but we have to assume it wasn't to achieve world peace. We know what they're capable of and there has to be a reason for it. Hell, if they'd opted for horticulture my bet is it would only be so they could learn how to dig a grave."

Sacha chimed in. "We know they're smart. They probably have money and as you said, we know what they're capable of. You put those three things together and it can't be good."

I nodded, then carried on. "The Darkweb proved useful in a couple of instances, I found stuff on there that simply doesn't exist anywhere else."

I picked up my file case and dug around in it. "For starters, I got their psyche evaluations and police interviews from it, plus, some bits and pieces about where they were held from arrest to secure units. Psyche stuff first."

I handed over the report I'd unearthed.

There are a whole load of characteristics and social influences child killers share. They don't feature in each and every instance but appear often enough to rate as noteworthy. They might come from an abusive home in impoverished communities suffering from a high crime rate, suffer from chronic family instability and/or from being bullied. They often have psychological disorders, for example explosive tempers. They tend to be loners prone to victimising younger, weaker kids. They might be influenced by graphic media. They can have sadistic personalities and get enjoyment from torturing and murder. This can be exhibited while still very young, usually featuring animals as victims. They might have an unusual physical appearance or psychopathic tendencies. This, and more, was in the preamble. But as far as these two were concerned, the report was guesswork and admitted as such.

There had been half a dozen or so interviews and all went the same way. They were sorry. It was an accident. I/We didn't mean for it to happen. I/We won't do it again.

Despite the examinations being held on an individual basis and that the twins hadn't been able to speak to each other since being arrested, they both recited the same mantra; reminiscent of a prisoner of war giving only their name, rank and serial number. Slight animation had been exhibited by both, only when their sibling came up in conversation. Those incidents aside, throughout the entire process of examination, their demeanour had remained calm, almost detached according to the Psychologist. The official diagnosis was that they were Sociopaths. But there was a handwritten page appended to the report, a footnote addressed to Detective Inspector Ames.

Stuart. The diagnosis attached is what is required of me and based only on what I am permitted to say due to there being no medical evidence to the contrary. However, I was uncomfortable throughout. They are enigmatic and sinister. The expressions of regret were an automatic response rather than emotional, and were served up in an identical fashion, having clearly been rehearsed beforehand and then stuck to like glue. Not only that, I believe that the twins were aware that their identical responses would elicit suspicion but simply don't care and state they are sorry only because for the time being, it suits their purpose, which would be to avoid being labelled as psychotic.

Unofficially, I believe them to be high functioning, sexually sadistic psychopaths but that would be an opinion unsupported by the examination results principally because they have skewed them. They have no remorse or understanding of how real people behave. I suspect, no, I know that their responses to me were their Plan B, that in the event of being caught this is what we must do etc. They are capable, indeed likely of repeat offending. Please don't quote me. Good luck.

"That didn't come out in court."

"No." I replied, "How could it? Imagine what Mummy would have done to the psychologist with her own, ever so different report, and her two, well-scrubbed little angels shining in the dock. All anyone had to go on that was undeniable, in your face, plain fact, was the video. In a sense, we should be grateful it existed."

"How about the interviews?"

"More of the same. They didn't act like normal kids. As a rule, sooner or later, when two or more are involved, one of them cracks, starts blaming the other, it wasn't me etc. Not these two. As the psychologist said, all they got was name, rank and serial number followed by, we're sorry, it was an accident, we didn't mean it.

You get the impression from police notes that it didn't matter which one was in front of you, the response was the same. They were detached, almost as if they were paying attention elsewhere."

"Telepathy?"

"Nope. I investigated that, just in case. As fond as people are of attributing strange coincidences to twinship, it's all anecdotal, not a jot of science involved. The twin thing is interesting though. For an altogether different reason."

"How so?"

This was the tough part, the unacceptable face of The Twins.

"Well, it's generally believed that twins, have a deep emotional connection. In this instance, given that we know they're the high functioning, sexually sadistic psychopaths of the report, and identical twins to boot, it's highly likely that theirs is the only emotional connection they have and because of that they have an intense sense of empathy, so much so that it can generate physical sensations such as pain if the other one is hurting. But if that's so, who's to say it doesn't work the other way?

This isn't pleasant to think about, but imagine when they're doing something together, something that gives them intense pleasure as an individual, if we assume those physical sensations are then felt by the other, how that magnifies when it's reflected back, and then back again, how it increases exponentially, bouncing between them like an echo. A perpetual, rolling orgasm."

Sacha was sitting there silently, emotionless, so this was as good a time as any to give her everything.

"My guess is that they're incestuous. I just can't imagine how they could be anything else. If that started when they were young, and remember, they've always shared the same room, so probably the same bed, then they most likely don't see anything as taboo. When fiddling with each other got a bit dull or wasn't enough, they looked elsewhere for their kicks and as long as they had each other to fall back on, an utterly reliable collaborator, they couldn't give a shit about anything or anyone else. It's all about them and their thing. I'd bet good money that Mummy knows about the bedroom shenanigans and wouldn't want it to become common knowledge around Knightsbridge. I have no idea what kind of weirdo she is, but we have to assume that somehow, she's involved, even if it's only knowing what she does about them and still doing her damnedest to get them off the hook."

"So now we know why."

"Yep. Not only that, if they haven't already, they'll do it again. We're doing the world a favour."

Silence sat heavy between us for a while, clouds outside crossed the sun, darkening the kitchen as if to match the mood within.

"I want to go home."

That was about as much as she could muster. I set her off ahead of me, secured the house, then followed.

The Jedi

Parking space had always been limited at the front of the house but there was a shared courtyard out back which gave her and her neighbours access to their garages. I'd driven through the archway and into the yard many times over the years and little had changed. I knew exactly where to go and slotted the Merc neatly in front of the garage shutter door. Once through it, there was a regular door at the other end which gave access to the garden, mostly given over to decking I'd installed years ago. I walked up to the glass patio doors and slid them open. Sacha seemed to have regained her composure.

"By the way, we have new neighbours."

"Really?"

"We do." Her voice hushed. "I think they're gay."

"Why are you whispering? It's just us."

"I didn't want to be rude, you know, tittle tattle. It's just an observation."

"Have they been there long?" I was just fulfilling my obligations to the conversation.

"Oh. Not long, just a few months. James was here on his own for a while then another guy, Ollie, turned up. They've been together ever since. Look, they're outside now."

I looked out into their garden. It sloped down and as they were at the bottom end, I could see over the fence. Two guys, similar build, slim, average height, could have been brothers but one had darker hair than the other. The fair haired one turned, handing the other an empty plant pot.

"Jesus! That's Pete! From the Hole!" I panicked and shot sideways away from the glass to put the living room wall between me and the view into the garden. I was trying to grab her arm to pull her away from the window. Sacha looked at me as if I was an idiot.

"You're kidding, right? Which one?" She was peering through the window despite my attempts to drag her back.

"The fair haired one. I'm certain of it. What's he doing here?" This didn't make sense. I'd only caught a glimpse of the guy but didn't doubt for a minute that it was Pete.

"But that's Oliver, or Ollie. The other guy is James."

Crouched there, ridiculous but fearful, wondering if Benny had somehow linked me to Sacha, I had no idea what to do next. Sacha took the initiative. "I'll pop out, say Hi."

"No!' I said urgently. That's fucking Pete! One of Benny's guys!"

"Well, it's no good hiding here. We have to do something. They've been here two months and I've yet to be murdered in my bed. I'm going out."

I was hesitant but she was right. Pete hadn't been a dyed in the wool Benny's boy, more a guy caught up in events. And making out he was gay? That wasn't the Pete I knew. My fear subsided somewhat as the logical part of my brain asserted itself. One way or another, this had to be faced up to and if necessary, we could always bolt for the country house. Having the run option and now that my initial fear and surprise were subsiding, I was also bloody curious. I straightened and nodded. "OK."

At the sound of our doors sliding open, Pete/Ollie looked up from his digging. "Mornin' Sacha. How's it going?" The other one, James, raised a hand in acknowledgement.

"Oh, fine." She said offhandedly. "We're a bit confused though."

"We?"

As casually as I could, and not feeling in the least bit confident, I walked out into the garden.

Pete saw me and smiled.

"Mornin' Tom."

There didn't seem much point in preamble. He knew me. I knew him.

"Morning Pete."

"Ah." He raised his arm, hand palm out, a gesture of peace. "It's Ollie, Ollie Jones, at least for now." He rested on the shovel. "This would probably be a good time for an explanation."

He wasn't in the least threatening. Quite the opposite, a wide grin on his face. "Wanna come round for coffee?"

"Nah. Don't think so."

"Relax, Tom. We're on the same side."

"Perhaps. But until I'm sure of that I'll stay right here, thank you."

"I can always hop the fence."

I got the sense I was being teased, rather than toyed with. "Don't do that. Who are you?"

"You remember engaging the services of a security company?"

I twigged. "You're Jedi?"

"What?"

"Jedi. It's what I call the security people. I never had an introduction, just a phone number."

"Ha! Jedi. I like it. Yeah, that's us."

I turned this over briefly while I sorted through my confusion. "So, you work for me?"

"Sort of. There's another party interested in your welfare. Between you, you split the tab."

"Christian?"

"Can't say. Goes against the creed. Anyway, we've been behind you most, if not all the way. How much have you told Sacha?"

"Everything."

"Fair enough, that makes life a bit easier. When you were scoping out the Hole and a few other joints, you were like a dog circling round on a blanket, trying to get comfy. 'Cos of that there were half a dozen of us tracking you, seeing where you'd settle, we kinda inserted ourselves all over town. James here got Peabody's. 'Cos I was in The Hole, I got the gig."

"And what gig was that?"

"To watch your back. We didn't have a clue what you were up to, weren't even sure you hadn't gone off the reservation, but I have to say it was the most fun I've had in I dunno when. You, Tom Hood, are one crazy motherfucker. Spending that twenty grand? Best job I ever had."

From the corner of my eye, I noted Sacha's expression change, perhaps at the suggestion that maybe I'd left something out and had more fun than was appropriate and not mentioned yesterday.

"Mate, if all you needed was a gun, you only had to ask."

"Ask who? Just who are you people?"

"We're the good guys. The other bill payer just wanted to see what would happen, what you'd do. Keep drinking or get on mission. We were tasked to find out and if it was the latter, help you along."

I was thinking on my feet now. The other bill payer had to be Christian. He used these guys and put me in touch with them, also, he hadn't resisted my suggestion that I might go after The Twins. It seems now that the cash wasn't completely philanthropic.

"He wants his own children dead?"

"Sneaky." He wagged a finger. "Neat trap. You're assuming the other bill payer is some guy called Christian. That 'aint something we can confirm."

He paused, then added, "I'll tell you though, that whoever you think this person is, their own security requirements are what we'd call excessive."

I let the identity issue go, Pete/Ollie, wouldn't confirm anything but on the other hand, hadn't denied it and my curiosity aside, it was pretty much irrelevant. Interesting, but irrelevant. I changed tack.

"You know I've broken a few laws and may be about to break others."

Ollie scoffed. "The law, what's that when there's no-one around?" He paused then answered his own question.

"As someone once said, rules are for the obeisance of fools and the guidance of wise men. Anyway, we never go in blind. At the initial briefing, when we were told it was you, we all knew something of your history. Any gaps that the newspapers had left out were filled in by our researchers. I don't think there wasn't one of us who didn't get a little bit mad at the way things turned out for you and your family.

As we see it, the law broke you and this is where you are, trying to deal with it. In this business, we tend to define the lines that others see as grey, clear away the crap…sometimes metaphorically speaking, sometimes with direct action. There was no shortage of volunteers for this one."

"Which of those apply now?"

"Well, we're just back up. For guidance if you ask for it. Perhaps even training We can't get directly involved. At least, that's what our brief is. Me, I'd be in there like a rat up a drainpipe. But that's up to you and off the books."

My curiosity got the better of me. "What happened after The Hole? That night?"

"Not a fuckin' clue. I knew you were up to something so tailed you. Watched you get in your car and leave. After that, it was easy. We found your car ages ago and bugged it."

I registered surprise, then annoyance. "Is the bug still there?"

"Course it is."

"Take it off."

"Can't do that. Against the creed. Gotta know where you are."

"I'll buy another car."

"And we'll bug it. Like I said, there's another interested party."

I let that go. "Is the Porsche bugged?"

"Yep."

"The house?"

"Both of 'em but only externally. Don't wanna intrude you know."

"Really?" I scoffed.

This place was getting crowded. My solo action had somehow been turned into a posse, a situation I was deeply unhappy with. I hadn't been comfortable about involving Sacha but for the sake of healing her and perhaps rebuilding our relationship, I'd overridden my doubts and it had become our thing; our make-or-break thing and anything else might somehow feel as if we had been cheated. I conceded though, given their commitment, that James and Ollie could prove useful. So, until I knew better, I put them in the credit column.

"What now?"

Ollie shrugged. "That's up to you I guess, but like I said, we're here to help."

I gestured towards the other guy, James, who up 'til now had remained silent, observing the exchange.

"Doesn't say much, does he?"

Ollie smiled. "Can't stop him once he gets started, He's the life and soul. Tom, meet James. Another Jones and a dab hand at housework, gardening and very useful in a tight spot."

I nodded. "Jones. A bit unimaginative. Not your real name I suppose?"

James spoke for the first time, in a soft, accentless voice. "Does it matter?"

"I suppose not." I shuffled on the spot, kicking a stray leaf off the decking. "Well, this is awkward. What are we supposed to do now? Do we hand over an itinerary and agenda?"

James spoke. "Not necessary Mr. Hood. You just carry on doing what you're doing, and we'll just get on with our job. We're watching your back. That's all."

I couldn't fathom if this were a blessing or a curse. Part of me was pissed off because I thought I handled The Hole solo. It turns out now that there might have been interference. That bases I'd thought I'd covered had perhaps been overlooked and taken care of by Ollie and his mates.

I needed to know if I'd fucked up anywhere and any mess had been tidied up behind me.

"Ollie," I'd have to get used to that. "tell me something. Those months in The Hole, is there anything I should know. I mean, did you have to do anything to clean up after me?"

Ollie's ready grin resurfaced. "Tom, I have to tell you, no. You were what you appeared to be. No-one thought anything else. All that time, edging your way in. Patient, careful. Then when you got in, the drinking, the parties, the weed, the coke, you never let your face slip. You were who you were and nothing about you suggested otherwise. I'd have had to break cover and move in if you had and let's face it, that didn't happen. I was just Pete. Divorced and fancy free. Like I said, best gig I ever had. You're a gifted amateur. You should see my report, not that it'll ever see the light of day. Good job, man."

I couldn't help the sense of satisfaction I felt. There are times when things we do have to go unnoticed and can't ever be spoken about, shared. But someone else was there. Had seen it. No matter how childish it might seem, the need for recognition had been met, I felt somehow validated.

I glanced across at Sacha who, like James, had taken little part in the conversation so far. There was a look on her face that seemed out of place given the subject matter. It was satisfaction.

"For the record," James interjected. "Peabody's was The Hole without any of its redeeming qualities."

I guessed that was James telling me I'd judged The Hole right for my purposes, and that felt good. Setting history aside, I turned to the present. "You mentioned help." I said, an idea forming.

Ollie and James exchanged a glance.

"Up to a point." James acknowledged. "What do you need?"

"How are the cars bugged?"

"It'd be easier to show you. You'd best come around." James again.

I looked to Sacha, this was really the beginning of it, and I wanted her to take the first step. "We'll be there in five." She replied. It was as simple as that, and I hoped that things would remain this uncomplicated. We walked back into the house.

"A couple of things first before we go round." I said. "Burn phones." Explaining their benefits, I continued, "We'll pick a couple up to use exclusively between us but remember, for normal stuff our regular phones have to be used. They're the first things the Police will confiscate if this fucks up so *reconciliation* texts and conversations take place on those. Keep it normal."

As an afterthought I added, "Unless they have a better idea, I'll pick up another to keep in touch with the neighbours. Ready?"

Sacha grabbed her coat and bag and headed for the door. "Come on, then." I closed the door behind me and followed her out.

Ollie let us in. Their place was a mirror image of Sacha's, but truth be told, tidier. Spartan but with clear evidence of being occupied there was a place for everything and everything in its place. I mumbled something complimentary.

"That's James." Said Ollie, smug.

James grumbled briefly about Ollie's lack of discipline around the house. "His room's a shithole, I can't live like that."

"Yeah, you'll make somebody a great wife someday." Ollie shot back.

"Get fucked."

I interrupted this domestic idyll. "So, gay? What's that all about?"

"Great cover." Said Ollie. "Ideal for going quietly go about our business."

James was at a small desk tucked away in a corner of the living room.

"Over here." He said, "This is more Ollie's thing, so I'll let him brief you. Anyone need a drink?" We asked for coffee and James made for the kitchen.

The three of us hovered over a laptop. "Two ways of doing it depending on the age of the car. First, there's the good old fashioned sticky bug planted on the car. But only old fashioned in how it's deployed. After that, both methods work in much the same way, via satellite links. The Porsche has the bug, your Merc though, well, we use the cars own systems to follow it."

My eyebrows furrowed, Ollie saw my puzzlement and continued. "You have a little red button in your car. In case of breakdown, you press it and good old Mercedes Benz know where you are and come out to fix you, right?"

I nodded.

"We just hack into that. It's never dormant, there's a constant feed of info about where you are and what the car's doing. We're only interested in where you are. This programme is the hack. There's another programme on here that follows the Porsche. Why? Who or what do you want to keep tabs on?"

I wasn't too concerned about letting that particular cat out of the bag. They were clearly breaking a few laws hacking systems and we had no nasty surprises planned for Mrs. Christian, we just wanted to follow her.

"We want to know where Mummy goes. See if that gets us to The Twins."

"Solid idea." James had come back with refreshments. There was a tray with biscuits and cups on saucers. Ollie's observation about James's eligibility was clearly spot on.

Watching them interact while we drank our coffee was an interesting exercise. Sacha and I occupied one sofa while they sat on another. They were going over the best way a couple of amateurs might successfully bug a target. James approached the subject seriously, thinking things through before coming up with a solution. Ollie was more reactionary, coming up with ideas then shooting them down himself when an obstacle presented itself. They worked together on the laptop, looking up CV's, addresses and maps. You could see how they might work independently of each other but that working together was a combination of two minds at work from different angles until an idea became workable and more to the point, achievable.

"OK." Said James. "You heard most of that but to clear the decks a little this is how you should play it."

Sacha and I hadn't moved from the sofa.

"As we know the target is London based. With that in mind there are two ways to approach this. The first is in plain sight. Regular people on a city break. But you can be tracked. If you go by car there are cameras and number plate recognition systems, mobile and static that will log you in a place and time. If you use credit cards, and you almost certainly will, there will be a paper trail. Regrettably, any future investigation might unearth your proximity to Mrs Christian and questions best avoided might be asked. We should inhibit that, which leaves us with one alternative. Covert, under the radar. Your choice."

James waited while we made our decision. It was a short discussion. Between the two of us, we reckoned the covert option to be our best bet. Firstly, because sniffing around Mummy in plain sight was a bad idea, as already stated by James, but our principal motive was to gain experience. The Hole had given me some expertise. But it would be new for Sacha and because in future, we might be forced to operate in that environment, it would be best to get used to the idea now, in a situation where no harm was intended.

"What does option two involve?" I asked.

"Good choice." He said, before outlining it and prior to our even agreeing it.

"You're certain to have to adjust your behaviour at some point so now is as good a time as any to start getting in the groove. Ok. You leave your cars and credit cards here, take plenty of cash. If you're asked for a credit card, which is only likely to be when booking into a place to stay, say you had your car stolen with everything in it. Travel light and buy everything new, as if that were the case. For that reason, you, Sacha, will not have a handbag and you, Tom, no wallet. Check the schedules then take a bus to a mainline train station, nothing small, pick a big one where you're least likely to be remembered. When you get to London, use buses and tube only, see the sights. Take your time, a few days at least, to get acclimatised to the city, try to blend in. Be grey. If you get lost or confused, keep going regardless. Whether you feel it or not, maintain an air of familiarity in your surroundings until you can find a logical, quiet place to stop and reassess". He paused, giving time for information to be absorbed.

"Her office is near a landmark or two and there's a coffee shop we reckon she must pass to get to work, for all we know, she may even use it. Buy a newspaper or magazine and give it a couple of mornings around rush hour to see if you can spot her. You can't make a habit of that though. Like I said, just a couple of mornings. When you've got her, you'll need to track her back to where she lives.

When you've got that far, it should be a snip to I.D. her car and if it's an old model, bug it. If it's new, we need the registration and if we're lucky, we can use a similar system to what's on your Merc. If not, well, like I said, you'll have to plant one, which is where it might get sticky. Sacha, how is your English accent?"

"I've lived here long enough and played around with it. I guess I can manage something convincing."

"Good," said James. "Start living it. An American stands out."

All this made perfect sense and would help us to avoid attention, but it crossed my mind that these boys had access to all kinds of information which would make all of this unnecessary.

"Don't you already know her address or isn't there a database that would have her registration? Wouldn't that be less risky?"

"We do and there is." James paused, thoughtful. "We're happy to help, but we're not going to do the job for you. To save time, but only for that reason, here are two clues to get you started. Her office address and she doesn't drive to work. That's all you're getting. Work it out.

This is about getting you into spy mode, making you think and if necessary, adjust on the hoof. You two need to start behaving as if you have something to lose. It might save your lives or worse, jail time. Call it tough love."

Ollie shrugged as if to say, *'If it were up to me?'* But James had a point and Ollie knew it, so it looked like we'd have to go the long way around on this one.

Sacha chimed in. "OK. London it is."

They asked us about our phones and nodded approval when I explained our arrangements. Secure numbers were exchanged in case of emergency. Having agreed to look after Pooh, Ollie printed up maps and addresses and handing them over, waved us off with, "Have fun, kids. I'm picking up some kit while you're away and when you get back, you're going into Boot Camp." Whatever that meant.

We spent the rest of the day picking up some ready cash from the country house, checking schedules and familiarising ourselves with maps and the location of Mummy's office. Mid-morning the next day, we left the old house on foot and headed for the bus stop on the nearby main road. It all felt so new and yet comfortably familiar with Sacha strolling beside me.

We'd walked this street together a hundred times. I almost reached out for her hand as we walked but then remembered that this wasn't the good old days. We carried nothing with us to indicate we were planning a journey, just the clothes we stood up in, phones, and pockets full of cash. Tucked away, but handy, we also had a couple of the sticky bugs.

I couldn't recall the last time I'd used public transport in general and buses in particular. Today, we were going the whole hog. A bus into Leicester, a train from there to Birmingham New Street and then a stroll across the city to Moor Street Station. There was a route from there that would take us direct into Marylebone, London. Sacha, thinking ahead, even had the right change for the bus, something that hadn't crossed my mind. The route into Leicester was a familiar one, we'd often driven it in another life but on this occasion, rather than having to concentrate on my driving, I was able to actually see all the sexy houses and parcels of countryside that over the years, Sacha had constantly and annoyingly pointed out to me when I couldn't take my eyes from the road and was therefore unable to join in the fun. Sitting back now, taking it in, I became more aware of how fortunate we'd been to have settled here. The occasional blot on the landscape aside, this really was a lovely part of the world.

Leaving the bus, the mile or so to the train station stretched our legs and sharpened our appetites, that said, our connection time was limited and the journey to Birmingham was a further hour, so we'd have to go without for the time being. New Street Station was a revelation having undergone a massive renovation. What before was dark, worn out, with an almost subterranean, Orwellian feel to it was now bright and modern and coming up and out from the platform was a pleasant surprise. There was the usual smattering of eateries, but they were now more glamourous than had been the case when I last used this place, maybe 20 years ago. So appealing in fact that we took some time to fill the gap in our stomachs.

Moor Street was an easy twenty-minute stroll away and as our journey thus far had been delay free, we were relaxed and chatty. This was all very novel and because of that, weirdly exciting.

Moor Street itself was a real eye opener. From the outside, it looked like a scene straight from the 1930's. Canopied over riveted iron supports, high arched windows set in red brick, it was absolutely not what I expected. Inside were more revelations, so much so, we picked up a booklet that described the renaissance that had taken place. Someone, somewhere, had apparently decided that the old, original building was just too historic to demolish and had made it their business to restore it.

What wasn't the refurbished original, was a sympathetic reconstruction. I half expected to see Trevor Howard and Celia Johnston in the café. Beautifully clean, there were large, mature potted plants scattered thoughtfully on the concourse. In a largely utilitarian world, the place was uplifting, refreshing, and a downright wholly unexpected joy. We took it in trying not to look too much like tourists as we waited for our train.

We knew the journey was a little under two hours. That would get us to Marylebone in mid-afternoon. We took the time go over what we knew. Mummy's offices were in Holborn, just around the corner from The Royal Courts of Justice, not to be confused with The Old Bailey, which is around half a mile east, closer to The City.

There were heaps of reasons for tourists to be wandering the area with Museums, Libraries, and old architecture in abundance, hopefully, disguising ourselves amongst them would be a breeze. There were hotels aplenty within a small radius and we'd scoped these out on the internet, finally choosing a variety we could book in and out of depending on how long our stay would end up being. We had no intention of being further than a walk away from Holborn or Temple, the two tube stations closest to her offices.

The Tube was certain to be a nightmare during rush hour, so we weren't going to be inside the stations themselves. Instead, we'd separate and skulk casually outside them, or if there was a coffee shop nearby, in the warmth, hoping to spot Mummy going into work. We didn't much fancy the idea of splitting up, but we had no choice.

During the day, we'd do what we'd always promised ourselves, See London. In the past, holidays had been sunseekers and short city breaks abroad. Taking advantage of my airline concessions, we did the usual stuff. Spain, Greece for the annual break. Prague, Rome, Paris, and the like for quick getaway weekends. I don't know why we hadn't seen London as an alternative. Millions of foreign tourists did and for good reason. London is alive with theatre, restaurants, history, and culture. In a sense, we were looking forward to it.

We left the train at Marylebone, another restored delight and strolled out into London. Madame Tussauds was nearby but promising ourselves a visit later in the week, strolled down to Bond Street and took the Central line to Holborn. Fifteen minutes later, we emerged into what was to be our zone of operations until such time as we'd clocked Mummy. Reviewing our hotel choices, we plumped for the closest. As we checked in, as Mr. and Mrs. Wood, the desk clerk sympathised over our recent misfortune.

"Oh, that's awful. Please don't let it spoil your stay."

We left a significant deposit in lieu of our stolen credit cards while praising Sacha's Mother who, bless her, we said, had forwarded us the cash to enable our holiday to continue uninterrupted.

Over the week or so it took, we did and saw as much as we could in what we called our *down time*, between rush hours. On foot mostly, using the Tube and buses to cover the larger gaps, we discovered another world and we found out more about each other with each day. Stuff that had passed us by when opting for the beach. Art, music, architecture, and tradition, all talking points, some of it quite passionate and animated, particularly when an element of Britain v the U.S. crept in.

Mornings and evenings were for business. There wasn't a coffee shop directly opposite Mummy's offices, so we used The Strand as our meeting point as it was roughly in-between the two stations we had to cover. Sacha took Holborn, I took Temple. We were both nervous. We couldn't afford to be seen by Mummy. If we got careless or unlucky even in something as outwardly mundane as exploring London, someone, somewhere would be made aware that we were somewhere we perhaps shouldn't be.

Doubtless she'd get some kind of injunction despite our innocent protestations and that would be that.

The whole *spy mode* thing was a difficult mantle to adopt but we got on with it. Learning and adapting as we went along. It was the morning of day three when we first spotted her. It was Sacha who'd made the call. My prepaid disposable buzzed in my pocket. I fished it out with cold fingers.

"I've got her. She's on foot and just going in now. Where are you?"

I told her and was already walking towards our pre-agreed coffee shop on The Strand.

"Get me a flat white. I'll be with you in a minute."

I ordered her a coffee as I waited, knowing she'd be ready for a warm. I'd got it back to the table as she came through the main door and spotted me, she was flushed, clearly excited. I gave her a look that said, *Take it easy, be grey.* She slowed in acknowledgement, relaxing as she made her way through the small queue that was habitual at any time of day. She sat, taking off her gloves and reaching gratefully for her coffee.

"It was her. No doubt." Sacha was trembling. I couldn't tell if it was excitement or fear.

In truth, Mummy was hard to miss, at least for us. I remembered her from the trial. A pinch faced bitch, tall, bony, and birdlike, skinny rather than slender, hair dark and spiked. She was way too old to be hanging onto that look, but it suited us, giving us another reason to not like her very much. *Mutton dressed as lamb.* Was how Sacha had graded her. I just saw her as a bitch, an opinion that grew with the way she'd brayed in court, defending her babies.

"No escort. On her own?"

"S'right. Bitch was in a crowd; coat collar up but that walk of hers and her hair? I'd know it anywhere. Trendy she 'aint."

"She didn't see you?"

"No, sir. I was on the other side of the road, walking away, just caught a glimpse of her in front of me."

Since arriving in London, I habitually carried a map of the Underground and fished it out now. She shuffled her chair around to study it with me. We were just a couple of tourists, wondering what to do with our day.

"Ok. Holborn has Piccadilly and Central lines running through it. We'll do it in stages. I'll stay outside to spot her going in, you wait by the ticket barriers to see which line she takes, buy an oyster card so you can go down to the platform.

Then we come away and leave it a day. Next time around, one of us gets on the train with her, when she gets off, we don't, we'll just get off at the next stop. We take the next day to recce and find vantage points to watch the station. When we're happy with that and see her exit, we follow. This could take days."

"I don't care." Said Sacha, warming her hands around her coffee cup. "Just seeing the bitch has me wound tight."

I thought about that for a moment then realised why we'd been sent to do this the hard way.

"James didn't say this, but I have an idea it was in his mind." I paused, getting my words right.

"He knew this would be a trip down Memory Lane. We have to see her not as what she was, but as she is right now. A means to an end, we must try to forget why. Develop an immunity."

Sacha thought that one through then visibly relaxed.

"It wasn't easy. Came as a shock, seeing her. I wanted to wring her scrawny neck, but I guess you're right. I'll be ok. Just give me a minute."

She looked over at the map again. "Natural History Museum?"

I got it. She was settling back into tourist mode.

"Sounds good to me. At least it'll be warm. Let's aim to be back at Holborn around three. See if we can catch her on the way home."

We spent the day relaxed, but not. Now we knew where Mummy had got into town, we had a focal point and were itching to see where that would take us. But Holborn was just the trunk of the tree, from there, we knew it would branch off, how many times, we simply didn't know. We'd just have to keep doing what we were doing until we tracked her home. We wanted to get this over with but knew that to do it safely, we'd have to stay low and be patient. It wasn't going to be easy, and I wondered bleakly how I'd react when I laid eyes on her for the first time since the trial.

Sacha stood. "Ready?"

The Museum didn't open til 10am but we reckoned that if we took in St. James's Park and the southern edge of Hyde Park, it'd be about ninety minutes on foot, and we'd land as the doors opened. Like all public museums in London, it was free. The money wasn't important, but the principle is, massive and fascinating, we stayed until about 2pm. Not nearly long enough to see it all but we had things to do. Footsore, we hailed a black cab and arrived in the area in plenty of time for a late lunch.

"Are you sure you'll be ok when you see her?"

"I'll have to be. That's why I asked you to be inside. Until it happens, I'm just not sure."

"You'll be ok, honey. You'll see."

I hoped so. It was time to move.

Like most underground stations in London, the façade of Holborn looks out over a narrow pavement, the road traffic separated from the pavement by a waist high steel fence. With Sacha now inside, I waited on the opposite side of the road, separated from the station entrance by around five lanes of traffic. I didn't feel too disadvantaged by that. Sacha had described what she was wearing, and Mummy's distinctive walk should be enough of a giveaway. I had a text for Sacha already prepared. All I had to do was thumb, *send*, and she'd be waiting.

Things went our way. I spotted her a mile off in an animated discussion with a suit. I'd never seen him before and hoped he'd be going into the station with her, as an added distraction to keep Sacha from being seen. I was curiously unemotional at seeing her. She was the object of my interest rather than the subject, separating it that way, just by changing a word in my head, made it somehow easier. They entered together and I hit the button.

On the way.

All I could do then was wait. I knew that Sacha had shopping bags with her that if Mummy got too close, she could bend down and rummage through them as camouflage but nevertheless, it was ten long minutes before she emerged. She knew where I'd be and without jaywalking, unhesitatingly made her way across the street.

"North on Piccadilly." She said simply, triumphantly. "I could do with a drink."

"You're not the only one." I replied. The short wait for Sacha was up there in my top ten list of the least fun I'd ever had in my life.

Showered, shaved, and smartened up. We were now de-stressing by experimenting in a trendy little cocktail bar. Cleverly, in the spirit of the moment, I ordered a 'Vesper', made famous by Ian Fleming. I soon wished I hadn't. How Bond drank that was beyond me. Sacha saw my distaste.

"That's my department, I think you'll find. White spirits and all that."

It had more of an edge of methylated spirit, so I slid it sideways across the bar, gladly exchanging it for something fruity and less deadly. Perhaps a little mean spiritedly, I noticed that even Sacha struggled to down it.

"So," She grimaced, swallowing my ex-cocktail. "We know which way she's headed and on what line. I guess now we need to get up close and personal." Sacha was right but I had an idea.

"As long as we're split up, we should be ok. If we put ourselves at different ends, it'll go some way to reducing the risk of being seen and recognised."

"Do you know what, Tom? I don't think she'd know who we were even if we sat next to her. Have you noticed how wrapped up she is, like in a little world all her own?"

I hadn't but then I'd only caught sight of her briefly.

"Let's hope you're right."

In the event, she was. Mummy was so familiar with her surroundings and routine, she seemed to insulate herself from her fellow travellers. She never so much as glanced around, eyes and body fixed with the sole purpose of getting home. We had her bracketed between us. The scrum in the carriages made it difficult to keep tabs on her. Difficult but not impossible. We watched her as she got off at Caledonian Road station. We got off at Holloway.

The next day was more of the same thing except having got there by cab, we were each stationed about a hundred yards either side of the Tube exit on the Caledonian Road, waiting to see which way she turned. It helped that she was a creature of habit. Sacha and I had agreed that if she turned my way, we'd give up tailing her for the time being and station Sacha there the following night. In London, in the dark, women can be nervous and aware of lone men behind them.

Our stay in London was prolonged in that that's exactly what happened. I let her walk by on the other side of the road and then strolled down to meet up with Sacha.

"She went thataway." I thumbed.

Sacha nodded.

"Tomorrow then."

We took in Chinatown that night, dining well, relaxed in each other's company. Conversation was limited by avoiding the subject of Ellen. We hadn't achieved anything yet and I guess it was too soon for either of us to reminisce. Though we'd been sharing the same room at the hotel, all the niceties had been observed.

We closed bathroom doors while showering and took care not to stray too close to one another. By acknowledging that we were just two people on the same track rather than a couple, it wasn't as awkward as it could have been. There was a good-sized chaise that served as a bed for me.

Two days later, after Sacha had successfully followed Mummy home the evening prior, we strolled past her house. Georgian, three storeyed and set back from the road, no driveways unfortunately, that would have been too easy. There were cars in the street, but we couldn't be sure which was hers. A Prius, an Alfa Romeo Spyder; if you're gonna break down, at least do it in style, Mercs, Volvos.

My money was on the Prius. It was parked central opposite the frontage and people have a way of declaring ownership of their favoured spot. Rush hour had been and gone, as had Mummy.

"I suppose we can be reasonably sure The Twins aren't in residence?"

There were no twitching curtains, no lights, nothing to indicate any signs of life. That aside, them being here, somewhere so obvious would have been utter madness. It was a safe bet that of all the places they could be, this wasn't one of them.

"That would be asking for too much." I replied. "But anyway, we need them to be somewhere quieter. Them being tucked away somewhere low profile is our best chance of getting at them."

We'd made our way down the full length of the avenue, mentally noting rubbish bins, postmen, and any obvious signs of security precautions. London was a city of perpetual motion, always someone about or awake. We couldn't hire a car. There was nowhere nearby for us to observe without being observed, no hotels with overlooking rooms, nothing we could use as a static vantage point, and we couldn't simply keep wandering up and down. We limited ourselves to one pass a day but sooner or later, we'd attract attention. Our problem then, was how to identify which car was hers and be there to see it.

"We need to set off the alarms."

"What?"

"It's the only way," I said. "We don't have a clue which is hers. If we set the alarms off late at night, owners will come out. Hopefully, she'll be one of them."

"How do you suppose we're going to do that?"

I didn't know but mulled it over. The road was packed nose to tail with parked cars, typical of residential London.

Sacha came up with something less drastic. "How about we just stick a blank piece of paper underneath the wiper blades? Only the owner will bother to remove it. We'll put them on half a dozen each side of the house."

"It's a better idea than playing knock and run. We'll do it tonight."

The next morning, we were playing at house hunting. There were For Sale signs dotted randomly about and we were at the far end of the avenue, her house in our line of sight. We jotted down Estate Agents phone numbers as any interested party might, taking our time, looking properties up and down all the while occasionally glancing towards the true object of our attention.

We knew roughly when Mummy would leave for work and had timed our approach carefully. Irritated owners saw the A4 sheets we'd planted on their windscreens late last night. Wet and fragile from the dew, they fell apart as they were removed. The more conscientious residents balled them up and binned them. Others were less environmentally friendly, dropping them in the gutter whilst shaking or wiping their hands dry.

We saw Mummy's door open and her closing it behind her. Perhaps we were fortunate but at that time, her next-door neighbour was engaged in removing the soggy mess we'd left on his windscreen and made a comment we couldn't hear. Mummy's attention was drawn to the Prius. Even at this distance, we could see her face sharpen as she picked her way across the pavement and daintily began peeling away at her windscreen.

Sacha and I looked at each other.

"Cracked it." I mumbled, ostensibly taking notes from a billboard.

She smiled, satisfied. "It looks new but let's not take any chances on it having GPS fitted, we'll bug it tonight."

We spent the rest of the day ambling around London, had lunch, killed time. I called the Jedi to let them know how things were going and that we'd be back some time tomorrow assuming things went well fixing the bug, they did.

You can never tell these days which parts of a car are plastic or steel. To cover all eventualities, the base of the bug had a strong, circular sticky pad surrounded by a magnetic ring. It was late but not too late to attract attention. House lights were going out as occupants turned in for the night, resting before starting another day in paradise.

Strolling by, briefly stooping, and fixing it inside the wheel arch was needlessly nerve wracking. It had taken a week, but we'd found her, tracked her home and the bug was fixed. We were quietly confident we'd done all of it without being compromised. Mission accomplished.

Boot Camp

"Ok. She's tagged. Now the fun starts."

"Question…What is the one thing you'd do if you *knew* you were going to succeed?"

We were back at Sacha's. James had sat us down and was leaning against the living room wall, arms folded. Looking intently at the pair of us. Everyone in the room knew the answer to that, *kill them*, so we waited for the moment of affirmation to pass.

James continued. "Then let's make sure that happens." He paused again, then his tone changed as he went in lecture mode.

"For the moment, we have no idea what kind of environment the targets are living in. If I had to guess, I'd say it's most likely to be rural, it's generally easier to keep a low profile and neighbours can be avoided or shut out by gates. You two are townies. That won't do. We need to tune you into the countryside, make darkness your ally. That, my friends, is the purpose of the next few weeks. The first thing we have to do is relocate to the country house, we need the privacy, grounds, gym and pool."

"I'll lay the gardener off."

"No need." Said Ollie.

I looked sideways at him, puzzled. Then slowly cottoned on. "Oh, fuck off. Please don't tell me he's Jedi?"

"Retired, sort of. Sorry."

I wasn't going to ask what 'sort of' meant. After getting over my initial feeling of being had, it felt weirdly comfortable at just how good these people were. Even at my most paranoid, Sid had never given me the slightest sense that he wasn't quite what he seemed to be.

"A bit of a legend, old Sid." Continued Ollie. "He was in Baghdad when I was in my dad's bag. Can't say too much, but I wouldn't fuck with him."

If I'd ever started to, this was where I would have given up trying to predict what else the Jedi might have up their sleeves. They were professionals, easy in what they did and how they did it. "Fair enough. Shall we?"

It wasn't difficult. The boys had a 4x4 already packed and we were told to bring just the one car. We took the Merc, Pooh, and his essentials in the back along with what were essentially overnight bags.

"You won't need much." We were informed, ominously.

When our convoy arrived, Sid was on the driveway, waiting. Getting out of the Merc, I strolled over and shook his hand. "Sid. You're an arsehole." Mindful of what Ollie had said, I made sure I smiled when I said it.

He grinned back. "No worries, Mr. H. Glad to be of service."

He spoke in an accent I hadn't heard him use before; one he'd hidden. That's when I figured out, he was actually Australian and that my glowing recollections of the Antipodes over tea and sandwiches had been listened to by a native, not an unworldly gardener. He registered my realisation with an infuriating smile, I'd been had. This place was turning into the United Nations.

Sacha took Pooh into the house and once he knew where his basket was, was let out into the garden. Emptying the Merc, Sacha and I waited in the kitchen. Our three Jedi strolled in. James put the kettle on and briefed us as it boiled.

"Right then. This is how it goes. You two have no idea what may or may not lie ahead. Nor, come to that, do we, and while we don't have the time or facilities to teach you everything you might need, we can prepare you for the basic stuff. You might think you're moderately fit. You're not. We're going to change that and once we have, we'll work on changing your mindset, take you out of the town and back to nature.

Think of this as an episode of 'I'm a Vigilante. Get me out of here.' You, Sacha, we reckon to be a top-heavy size twelve. You'll be a ten when we're through." For some reason, she smiled.

"You, Tom, are flabby." I felt offended, I might not be as fit as this pair of racing snakes, but I still worked out and felt pretty good for an old 'un.

"There are kitbags in the back of the Landie, one for each of you. Some of it will need to be broken in, as will you. Sympathy…don't expect it or ask for it. For the next few weeks, or as long as it takes, the only place you're going to find it, is in the dictionary, between shit and syphilis. Get settled in, get a good night's sleep. We start first thing tomorrow. Alarms set for 5am please."

I couldn't see much reason to be smiling, as Sacha had. Having been a reservist, I had a vague idea of what to expect and wasn't looking forward to it.

When I'd bought the house, I no idea it would be turned into some kind of wartime commando training centre. But that, essentially, is what happened. Not outwardly, no assault courses, muddy pools, or rope walks but in its intent.

As bid, at 5am the next morning, we were up, dressed and waiting downstairs in the kitchen, self-conscious in our brand-new gear looking for all the world like a pair of apprentice terrorists. James came in, he had the look of a man on a mission.

"Right!" He clapped his hands together, rubbing them vigorously. "In the interests of health and safety, a full and comprehensive medical first. Eyesight and hearing, all ok?" We nodded.

He went on. "Flat feet? Arthritis? Hideous tropical diseases?"

Sacha and I shook our heads to indicate we suffered from none of those.

"Anything at all anyone wants to tell me?" He paused; hands spread to emphasise the question. I didn't see much point in mentioning my repaired hip. They either already knew about it; which seemed most likely, and it would hold up, or it wouldn't. He took our silence to mean that all was as it should be or at least, we hoped it was.

"No? Excellent. Then let's get to it."

An hour later, we were covered in mud, ragged and panting, bent double in a forlorn attempt to get our breath back.

I couldn't remember my own name and Sacha, despite regular dog walking, fared no better. I was shocked to discover that my gym hours had done nothing for my stamina. On that first cross-country run, I was hanging out of my arse within a mile. We ran in boots and James had been right, some of the kit needed breaking in and footwear was no different.

For days we blistered, bled, gasped, groaned, and sweated but as time passed, to our surprise and no small relief, were managing better as we healed or overcame the pain of the new regime. Sacha and I had always been competitive. Monopoly and Trivial Pursuit were games we'd played only once, at least against each other, the fallout from the result making it simply not worth the grief. But that competitive streak motivated us far beyond our physical abilities as we found ourselves accepting and fighting silent challenges. We had a sneaking suspicion that there was a psychologist in James that saw this and used it against us, but that was ok. We all had a common aim.

When we weren't running or doing press ups, we were being familiarised with night vision kit, communications procedures and stripping and reassembling the Glocks, Ollie having brought the 'spare' he'd lifted from Benny. Now that we had two of them the question as to who would carry our only gun had been answered and, in a sense, equalised our status as a team.

It took a while, but eventually, the strip and reassemble could be done blindfolded and in good time and each of us recognised our own weapon simply by the feel of it. Inside two weeks, boots, feet, muscles, and lungs came together and with that, a sense of achievement. Of being stronger, more able.

My repaired hip held up well, I was never going to move with the speed of a tall Indian as in my youth, but we were easily covering five miles and at the end of it, were it required of us, felt we could do five more. We were never going to be superhuman but as James had once explained, that wasn't what this was about. We weren't expecting to have to tab twenty miles day after day, SAS style. We just needed to be fitter and stronger than we had been.

Before this part of our training had started, as fit as I thought I was, it turns out that the only part of my body that was getting harder, were my arteries. Not true anymore. Our clothing was functional, a dull black, and became almost a second skin, after runs, we'd swim in it, boots and all. The pool was going to need a serious clean sometime soon, particularly as Pooh had decided he was now some sort of born-again gun dog.

I also suspected that the Jedi had added a little something of their own to the water, just to make it interesting. Simply looking at the pool made Sacha heave.

For her, the reality of having to swim in it took an effort of will. Not for me. I was 5'10'' and would happily have waded through a six-foot-deep pit of runny shit if The Twins were on the other side.

On the plus side, James did all the shopping and cooking and was seriously good at it. That said, by mealtimes we were invariably ravenous and much of it didn't touch the sides on the way down. At the beginning of week three, we were sat around the dining room table.

"We've been keeping tabs on the Prius. Nothing dramatic on that front. As for where we are right now, you've done the hard work and I have to say, I'm impressed. More to the point, injury free. We'll keep it up but to a lesser degree from here on in. Time for some fieldcraft. That's Ollie's specialty and goes some way to explaining why his room is such a shithole."

Ollie stood. It was his thing. He liked to move around the room when talking, expressing himself with body movements and sweeps of his arms.

"Lady and Gent, welcome to my world." He paused for dramatic effect, fully engaging us.

"Humans have an irrational fear of the dark. If it's of any comfort to you, it stems way back, to prehistoric times. Human eyes aren't adapted to the dark in the same way as the animals that used to hunt them, so man hid, tucked away in a cave somewhere. Kids, nowadays, thanks to evolution, deforestation, extinction, and much more besides, there is nothing out there that is going to stalk, kill and eat you". He paused but stayed on theme.

"In the woods, graveyards and alleyways, those noises you hear that give you the shits? Badgers, foxes, Tibbles the pussycat out for a midnight stroll, nothing more. Get used to that mindset. Make the dark your friend. It will hide you, keep you safe from prying eyes. Use it. Don't fear it. If, as we reckon, the targets are rural, there's every chance you're going to have to spend a night or three laid up nearby, watching, gathering intel. Noise…don't make any. If you're stung, cut, or knocked about in any way, hold it in. You'd be surprised how quickly you can develop that discipline. Hopping about squealing, *Oh shit, Oh shit!* when pain strikes is not how we skulk in the jungle. For the next couple of weeks, you're going to live in the grounds. You'll have sleeping bags, but that's it. Make your own shelter, I don't care how you do it, you'll learn from your mistakes, particularly the first time you get pissed wet through with no way of getting dry.

No showering, washing, shaving or changes of clothes. What you're stood up in now, you'll still be wearing when this part of your training is over."

Sacha immediately thought of her legs. She'd have to forego her nightly ritual of naked body butter. Then it got worse.

'You will shit into plastic bags and piss into bottles. It's chock full of DNA, not something you want to leave behind so you will store and bring it out with you. Decide for yourselves how you're gonna wipe your arses. No bog roll in the wild but whatever you use, that also comes out with you."

He handed us a transparent bag. Inside we could see more of the same and the bottles he'd mentioned. Thoughtfully, there was also a funnel. I guessed that wasn't for me. Sacha blushed.

"You'll itch for the first few days. After that, you're gonna start to stink. Don't worry about it. It's gonna be worse for us than it is for you. There is method in this. Wildlife can track a human being a mile off. Scented soaps, perfume, after shave, washing powder, all these things linger on you long after you think they've worn off. So, get used to it. Revel in it if you like. Now go outside and find somewhere out back where you can see the house, but not be seen, and dig in. Kids, we're going back to nature." There was delight in his final expression.

All we had were the clothes on our back, a sleeping bag apiece and a notebook and pencil. No instructions. We picked a hedgerow, about sixty metres from the house and embedded ourselves. 24/7 we chinned it out, fashioning a primitive shelter from branches and bracken. It took a bit of patching but eventually, it held off the worst of the rain, unseasonally, this was of the constant torrential variety that in the past, had caused Arks to be built.

Uncomfortable, wet, cold, we'd lurk in our hide taking two-hour stints on watch. The first night out we'd both been asleep until Sacha was woken with a boot in her back and the sight of Ollie with a vicious knife gleaming dully at my throat. *Learn.* Was all he said, before disappearing silently into the night. From that point on, one of us was always awake.

Lacking any other reason for being given it, we used the notebook to log movements around the house and grounds. Neither of us were wearing a watch, a rookie mistake so we had to guess at when stuff was occurring and took to describing the time in relation to the sun or moon, dawn or dusk. When Ollie saw what we'd been doing, he grunted in satisfaction, clearly that was why it had been issued, rather than for playing hangman or tic tac toe when we got bored.

In daylight hours, Ollie would teach us the basics of fieldcraft, how to use the ground as cover, how to choose a route by day, that we would then try to follow after darkness fell and then find our way back to the hide before sunrise. We were fed, which was nice. The sole reason for that, we were told, was that if or when we did this for real, we wouldn't be out long enough for food to be major problem, nutrition bars and dried fruit would be sufficient for our needs. Ollie was right about much else. We itched, then stank, then got used to it.

It was worse for Sacha than it was for me, but that's only because she was a girl and a fastidious one at that. Our clothing and sleeping bags took on a rank odour, then a personality all their own. We'd grin at each other through the grime because truth be told, the ordeal was almost fun, but swore an oath that when this was over, we'd never go on a camping holiday.

We learned to co-operate, look out for each other, do small things that mattered and as alien as it was, this time together did something to us. Things weren't as they had been, we weren't in the same bed, we were in a hedge but strangely, it was the experience we were sharing that was doing something to us, for us. We had to occupy the same, limited physical space.

Hands had to be offered and taken to overcome falls or obstacles. Touching became easier, no longer tentative but welcomed. We grew used to sharing body warmth, finding comfort where there was none. We laughed more, quietly of course, suffered more and through it all became more than we had ever been before, initially as individuals but gradually, as a pair.

The second week began with the handing over of a mean looking air rifle and instructions that night-time was now for hunting.

"You've had a week to tune into your surroundings. Now I want you to get used to having a lethal weight in your hands. This is only an air rifle but nevertheless, at short range, deadly. You will keep it clean. You've got too many rabbits, time for a cull. This exercise has a dual purpose. Firstly, to see how much fieldcraft you've absorbed. To get close enough to kill a rabbit with one of these you'll need patience, concentration but most of all, the ability to stay silent and if you miss, well, you'll have to start all over again, so take your time. If you can master all that, stalking a human will be a doddle. Secondly, you need to get your brains used to the idea of killing.

Mr. Bunny is cute and harmless but nevertheless must be taken down, he is your enemy, your target, you need to be able to look him in the eye and know that by pulling the trigger, it's goodnight. It's only a small step but will help, if and when, the time comes."

I couldn't see how shooting rabbits was any kind of preparation but was willing to accept Ollie's word. He noted my scepticism.

"Trust me on this, Tom. I'm restoring an edge that civilisation has taken from you. It's not about the rabbit. Your hatred of those two might, just might be enough to see you pull a trigger on them, but this is about removing the passion and replacing it with purpose. On seeing what's in your sights only as a target, nothing else. Your job is to get close enough to point, take aim and fire without missing. Nothing outside of that can creep into your mind."

Grimly, I nodded.

That night, as we left our hide and took to the woods, I was astonished at how normal our surroundings now seemed. Ollie was, yet again, right. The reconnaissance exercises of the first week had served us well. Not only were we able to sense more of our environment and discount what was natural, we also instinctively understood where the other was and could communicate with just a glance.

We were wraiths. This was cowboys and Indians writ large.

Sacha beat the crap out of me in terms of sheer ability with the rifle. I'd hit maybe two in five. There was nothing wrong with my fieldcraft, I could get close enough, but I just didn't have that certain touch with the weapon that she had. She never missed. Not once, and there were mealtimes when I wished she had. I was getting sick of rabbit. Rabbit corpses, still twitching and needing a mercy stroke, rabbit stew, rabbit fricassee, rabbit hotpot. Then, at last, on what we guessed to be day eighteen, a reprieve.

Until now, all our meals had been taken outside but today, in the late afternoon, we'd been called indoors to the kitchen. There was an odd sensation just crossing the threshold. After more than a fortnight in the undergrowth, we were almost wary of being indoors.

"Jesus, Mary and Joseph."

I turned and saw Sacha checking herself out in the wall mirror. Not having considered our appearance for some time and absolutely no care having been lavished on it, I saw immediately what had caused the outburst. We stank, we knew that, but any thoughts of personal image or hygiene had gone by the wayside when out in the bush.

As a description, bedraggled rural urchin might be a starting point, that's without considering that we were probably no longer alone in our clothes; Ollie had been right about the itching. But whatever might be lurking on our skin in terms of bugs and grime, it was her hair that stood out, in more ways than one. The once immaculate bob was a mess. Twigs, undergrowth and more besides stuck out in a variety of angles and combined with the dirt on her face, gave her the aspect of Inspector Clouseau following a bomb blast. She saw me in the mirror's reflection.

"Carla's going to kill me."

It had been a weekly ritual; one she clearly still underwent. Every Friday a stroll down to her hairdresser for whatever it was hairdressers did. It had evolved into more than a beauty treatment or business transaction and Carla probably knew more about Sacha than I did.

"I'd told her I was away for a few weeks so she wouldn't assume I'd been kidnapped, but how do I explain this?" Tangled, filthy hair caught between her fingers as she tugged and teased. I had no answers for her.

James rode to the rescue.

"Waste not, want not." Said James, dressing a bunny by the sink. I groaned inwardly.

"Sid's on his way round so it's Indian tonight. Incidentally, after that you'll have to have some time off before we do it all again. Rabbits have a way of knowing if you've had a curry. If I were you, I'd do us all a favour and get out of that minging gear and take a shower."

A now skinned bunny in hand, James turned from the countertop and as if looking over spectacles scanned Sacha up and down ruefully. "The pool is clean. Have a swim. The night is our own. Beer, methinks."

Sacha and I looked at each other. There was no need for a race, there were two fully fitted bathrooms in the place, but we both knew that a race was on, nevertheless.

"It's my fucking bathrobe." I menaced.

"Not if I get there first."

She was off and running, out of the kitchen and pelting up the stairs two at a time. I had more chance of plaiting snot than I did of catching her and there was the added distraction of her tight butt going up the staircase. Disregarding that it was clearly a lost cause and in the spirit of the chase, I launched myself after her. I got to the landing as I heard the bathroom door locking.

"Got it!"

I heard a muffled but triumphant cry through the woodwork. I wasn't going to look very vigilante like in fluffy pink. I hoped I had a clean track suit somewhere.

The rabbit curry was astonishingly good. James's cooking could be weird in one respect in that he spiced meals up with Turmeric wherever and whenever he could, promising that it worked on inflammation from within. I didn't doubt him, he'd daubed all manner of concoctions on various small injuries we'd sustained. He talked us through each treatment, how and where to find them in nature and all of which had been beneficial despite our scepticism.

It felt good to be clean, really clean. When I'd pulled off my gear in the bathroom, my face and hands, filthy as they were, were an entirely different colour to the rest of me, which had paraded a dirty, grey hue.

Sacha had gin and tonic, heaped with ice and a slice. Though clean at last, she was still running her fingers through her hair, unconvinced it had been partially restored. Beneath the hem of my robe, her legs gleamed, and I caught the faint scent of body butter. The boys and I had beer. Summer had gone and the nights were drawing in with a chill in the air. The fire in the hearth had been lit and we manoeuvred chairs around it to get the benefit of its warmth.

Ollie broke what had been a comfortable silence. "So, how has it been for you?"

Now there was a question that for me, was not a one sentence answer. I thought back to the loneliness of my pursuit and reflected on how much things had changed. How much I'd changed. Physically, I was a Spartan warrior, lean, muscled, flexible, ready. Mentally, I didn't know where to start and had so much to chew on that it was actually easier to sum it up in two words. Positively charged. Emotionally, I felt steady, calm almost. I couldn't remember the Tom Hood that had lain broken in a hospital bed. I didn't want to remember him.

Sacha spoke first. "I'm different. Good different. A couple of months ago, if anyone had told me I'd be sitting here with broken fingernails and scabs on my arms feeling proud of them, well…you know."

Eyes turned to me, and I felt the beginning of tears. It was at that moment that I knew what I felt. Gratitude and a sense of belonging. How could I express it? I struggled, trying to find a way to tell them what all this had meant to me. "I…I feel…grateful. If that makes sense."

There was a pregnant moment as if I was expected to deliver more. But I couldn't. The English language, for all its virtuosity, simply didn't have the words and without them, I couldn't translate what bubbled inside me.

Sacha reached over, placing her hand over mine. I think she got it.

She looked over at the Jedi and asked, "Why have you done this...helped us so much?"

Glancing briefly at each other, it was Sid who answered for the group. Leaning forward, his elbows on his knees, hands clasped together, almost in prayer, in a voice mellowed by compassion he said, "You're good people. Lord knows what that little girl could have become if left alone, to grow with you."

He allowed the memory of Ellen to sit with us for a moment then continued.

"Drug Lords, Despots, they're a known quantity and governments, organisations, people like us exist to eventually sort them out. But your little girl, you two, who steps up for her, for you? Everyone knows what happened in that courtroom." He let that hang.

"So, to us, it was simple, a choice between good or bad, often not a luxury our line of business allows. One way or another, one of you would have tried something, possibly failed, and ended up in jail, or worse.

Helping you good people was the right thing for us to do."

The three of them faced us, silent and understanding. Hard men carved from violence and conflict, there for us. I for one, felt humbled.

"What now?" I asked. I'd fully expected to be out in the rain tonight. I felt not a shred of disappointment.

"Well, from our point of view, it goes something like this. You've grafted. Done everything that was asked of you. Pushed yourselves. So as far as we're concerned, none of this has been a waste of time. Your training's over. We've got something for you. Call it a graduation gift." James nodded to Ollie.

Reaching behind his armchair, Ollie picked up two small packages, stood and handed one to each of us. Someone had taken the time to gift wrap them, albeit plain brown paper and tied with string. We opened them together. In each we found a military watch, a shoulder holster, and an identical pair of black leather gloves, again military issue, padded on the back of the hand and each finger. All bar one, the trigger finger. Symbolic.

Ollie spoke. "The watches and gloves speak for themselves." He paused. "I'm not a huge fan of shoulder holsters but in this instance, they have a place.

We're not talking about a concealed carry, if you're caught armed, you're stuffed anyway. This is about accessibility. You're both right-handed so I've set them up that way, we'll tailor them later. You won't be getting into any gunfights but may need to get to your weapons quickly. Not always easy, particularly when sitting or lying down, as you will be in your hide. You'll instinctively know where your guns are and how to get to them. You'll practice using these until it becomes second nature. You will keep them clean, with only one weapon stripped at a time. Being proficient in arms gives you an edge. Let's hope it's not needed."

Sid proposed a toast. "Raise your glasses Lady and Gents." He paused until we were all in the pose required. Then meaningfully, almost spiritually said, "Their time… is up."

Sacha and I glanced at each other, each understanding where we were, why and how good it felt. I tipped my glass gently in her direction, a salute she acknowledged. We drained our glasses then, to lighten the moment, upended them atop our heads.

That broke the mood, which lightened. More drinks were poured, and the evening developed from there.

The Jedi exchanged war stories, most of which were eye openers to us but brought scathing comments from each other.

Good natured stuff between peers. Scars were exposed and their origins explained. Sid had an impressive pair of feet, lacking several toes.

"Everest." He explained. "Adventure training, they said. Took me two tries but I got there."

Ollie stripped of his shirt, there were scars from what appeared to be claw marks. "Panther." He said. "Fucking great big Black Panther."

James almost choked. "Panther my arse. That was a junkyard Doberman. Columbia. Medellin Cartel operation. I told you it was a shit place for a rendezvous and," James wagged a finger, "you were only supposed to be there as an observer."

Ollie grinned. "Ok, maybe it was only half panther but fuck me it was big." He paused. "And vicious. A proper vicious bastard."

"How about you James?" Asked Sacha. "Any war wounds?"

"Nah. Too careful. I am, as they say, a perfect specimen."

"Wives, girlfriends?"

"Ollie's had the wives and Sid's in-between engagements, so to speak." James had artfully avoided the question, his private life it seemed, was exactly that. Private.

Stung by the 'wives' comment, Ollie struck back. "He's got a girlfriend. A dancer. Millie. No idea what she sees in him. I mean, if you ignore the cooking, cleaning and gardening skills, what use is he?"

"Ollie. You will never, ever understand how highly those talents are regarded by the fairer sex. It's enough to say I have a girlfriend, you have ex-wives."

"What does she say about your long absences?"

James paused, thoughtful.

"You're not gonna let go, are you?"

Sacha shook her head. "No Sir, I'm not."

He sighed. "We get together when we can. She has her thing, I have mine. Both of which are important to us. There'll come a time when we meet in the middle. Will that do?"

Sacha nodded but I could see she was only partially satisfied. She set her sights on Sid.

"Australian eh, Sid?"

"Yep. Here we sit, two strangers in a strange land, surrounded by philistines and barbarians."

"Have you thought about when you're going home?"

"This is my home." said Sid. "Unless we're up against the Poms in the rugby or the cricket." Quickly, he added, "I've got an Aussie flag somewhere, that's when it gets an airing. You?"

Sacha sat, staring into her gin, which had diminished somewhat. "My folks are dead. Have been for a while now, so as for going home, well, you know where it is, you guys' live next door. What's a girl not to like?"

Then we got to where I figured Sacha had been heading all along.

"Ollie. Tell us about The Hole."

I groaned inwardly. Not that I hadn't told her everything, it's just that after finding out Pete/Ollie had been there all the time, it had taken the shine off it for me.

Ollie grinned, reminiscing. "Best job I ever had."

"Is that it?"

"To paraphrase my learned colleague over there." Ollie gestured towards James. "You're not gonna let go of this are you?"

Her response was similarly repetitive. "No, Sir. I am not."

Ollie hunched forwards, his drink between his knees, looked Sacha straight in the eye and quietly, seriously said,

"Sacha. I did heaps of stuff there I should be ashamed of. But I'm not, truth be told, it's their world and all I did was react to the environment. Tom, on the other hand, and I guess this is what you want to know, Tom, is a good man, in any sense you want to interpret that. He had a job to do and did it. He may have broken a head or two but no hearts. Here endeth the lesson."

Sacha smiled, touching Ollie gently on the hand.

After that, the evening meandered pleasantly on but eventually, tiredness overcame us. The last eighteen days of two hours on, two hours off had left us bone weary and in need of a proper night's sleep. A few drinks hadn't helped, and we were shot. We said goodnight to the Jedi and climbed the stairs. Our rooms were opposite each other down a narrow corridor and as was usual, I wished Sacha goodnight and reached for my door handle.

She took my arm and softly said, "Not tonight."

Taken by surprise, I let Sacha lead me through her bedroom door. Her curtains were open, and moonlight cast a subdued lunar glow through the window. Closing the door behind her, she turned and faced me.

"Don't read too much into this, Tom." She said, taking my hands in hers.

"But I think after the last couple of weeks, I'd miss you tonight but more than that," she hesitated for a moment then, shrugging my ratty old robe from her shoulders, added conspiratorially, "I could really do with some good, old-fashioned sex."

Unselfconsciously nude, she stood there, waiting. I was numb. I'd grown so used trying not to think of her in this way that when the moment came, now, I was too stunned to react. She reached for me, pulled my tracksuit top over my head, then knelt and slid down the bottoms. Standing, she stepped back looking me up and down and offering me the chance to see her. Now alive to what was happening, I took it. Looking at her, there was no doubt that she was a simply fabulous creation, What God had given her, the last few weeks had enhanced. Her skin, burnished by moonlight, shone like an art deco statuette. The dips and curves of her body were defined by thrown shadows and were an irresistible invitation. As I absorbed my daydream, I knew that I would sell my soul to spend the rest of my life with this woman.

"Wow. Just look at us." she smiled. "It might be my memory, Tom. But I don't think you've ever looked better."

"You," I could barely speak. "Are breath-taking."

Part of me recognised that I was lost; she seemed out of focus, as if I couldn't quite make contact with her. Then, with what felt like relief, I realised I was being led towards the bed. I felt a rush of adrenalin, then a luxurious arousal reminiscent of our first time together, the years had fallen away, and we were back in time. I knew somehow that her gaze had come back to my face and her eyes were unerringly fixed on me. They stayed that way as we lay down together. My fingers reached for her hair, their actions separate from my will, a sensation of silk in my hands. My palms moved to her face, gently lifting it to my own and our lips brushed. Light, moist, sensual, releasing a desire that that for years I'd kept caged. A charge of nerve tingling expectation ran rampant down the length of my body, and I felt myself tremble with longing. She was utterly irresistible, once a part of my dreams but now a physical presence, a being my heart longed to cherish.

The outside world meant nothing now, my eyes closed, and I was oblivious to everything but Sacha. Our mouths pressed together with feverish haste. We had a need for each other, a pure heat that burned, demanding we touch. She took my hand and pressed it hard between her breasts, she held me there, almost willing me to feel the emotions surging beneath her skin as her heart beat faster.

My mouth moved to her neck, trembling fingers caressing, remembering, savouring the softness. The soft slope of her breasts guided my fingertips until they reached their goal. My thumb and forefinger closed, encircling the tip, hard with anticipation and desire. She shuddered, knees drawn together, her toes stretching, curling. Her head was thrown back, eyes tightly closed, her mouth open, pink tongue captive between teeth and lip through which breath was urgently drawn in shallow gasps. Her skin gleamed from the heat of passion and the reflection of the moon. My eyes lingered, overwhelmed by the sheer perfection of her exquisitely formed breasts that rose and fell with an erotic innocence all of their own.

I became aware of her hands on me, small urgent fingers touching, stroking. Her eyes flashed open, ablaze, entreating, wanting. Above all, wanting.

I fell on top of her, our skin moistening instantly as it touched, our limbs running together in the pale light. She found my hand again and demanded it between her legs, pressing her palm down, squeezing her thighs; she locked my hand into its soft prison. My fingers searched, found the wetness, dipped and moved up, bringing with it soft oils to heighten the touch.

She writhed beneath me, arching her hips upward, groans escaping, whistling hoarsely from her throat. She pulled the tormenting hand away, frantic to halt this attack on her senses.

Wanting, not wanting, the sensation too exquisite.

"Please."

Half heard but compelling.

Her mouth opened wide, soundless as I entered her. I heard her gasp as the invasion thrust fully home. Moving slowly, I savoured the sensation of being there. I filled her, emptied, filled. The rhythm established; her body moved instinctively with mine. I couldn't have stopped now even if I'd wanted to. Heaving frantically together, the tempo broken, I came. I felt the warmth of her as she flooded, heat coursing deep between us, touching every nerve, releasing me from reality, striking sparks from my brain, my head ablaze with light and colour.

Slippery with sweat, we lay together, the warmth of our exertions draping us. Sacha's breathing changed and I sensed that she wanted to say something.

"That wasn't just sex, was it?"

I knew these past weeks had brought us closer together, I just didn't know how close. But lying next to her, knowing that what was in me needed to come out, I was apprehensive but unafraid of what I knew I had to say. Never before Sacha, and certainly never after had I felt so at one with a woman. She was my friend. I had no trouble saying the words.

"I love you, Sacha. Always have, always will."

Sacha sighed deeply, contentedly, then held me tighter.

"That needs an answer, Tom." She shifted slightly, resting her head on my chest. I could feel her breath on my skin.

"I've told you I never stopped loving you, but there's a difference between that and being in love with you." She paused, then summed up her doubts, her words coming softly, thoughtful.

"And that's the thing. Who are you? There's the man you were before Ellen died. A loving, caring, wholesome man. There's the man you became, introverted, frantic, suicidal. And there's the man you are now, who I reckon has yet to fully reveal himself. Which one is you, the real you? I know it's been complicated, hell, I'm complicated, people just are, but there's a confusion here, something I can't commit to until I know. There are things about you I need to forget and things I need to learn. As for what we're doing…If ever I needed to justify it, what we plan to do, it's us. You were lost to me, Tom. As lost as Ellen was but this, it's bringing you back. And that has to be right, doesn't it? That we find something left of our old selves and remember what we shared?

I'm here, Tom. I'm here with you now and unless something happens to change the way my feelings are moving, I plan to stay, there's never been anyone else, I don't think there ever could be, but I just need to know. Be certain. I'm talking about the rest of my life."

She'd tensed as she'd spoken but now that she was done, visibly relaxed.

As I lay there, I thought about what she'd said. *Which one was I?* Drowsy, my thoughts faded. The last thing I remember before falling asleep was that for now, the man I am was going to see this through, wherever it went.

The Twins

"Morning, lover." She murmured, stroking his hair, sensing he was almost awake. He stirred and opened his eyes, blinking.

"Morning." He raised himself slightly, stretching, shaking off sleep. "What time is it?"

"Doesn't matter, does it?"

"S'pose not." Nevertheless, he turned his head to look at the bedside clock. It was a little after 10am. Early for them. "What did you wake me up for?" He grumbled.

Raising herself up on one elbow, she stroked his chest, raising the hairs on his chest between two fingers. "You need to start shaving them off. I don't like them."

"Mmmm? Oh. Yeah. Whatever."

"We need to start thinking about our big day, sleepy. Would you like some tea?"

"Yeah. Good." He rolled over and closed his eyes as she shuffled off the bed. He could vaguely hear her rummaging in the kitchen and then the creak of her footsteps on the stairs. Setting his tea beside him, she climbed back in beside him. She snuggled up, stroking his neck to soften his mood and continued where she left off.

"It won't be long now. Mummy promised." She wiggled her right leg, the tag annoyingly tight.

Awake, he rolled around, and she settled into the crook of his arm.

"We can't get straight into it, you know. Even when they take them off, they'll still be watching. And there's that cow from probation."

"I know." She said. "But we're moving along. Aren't we?"

"S'pose." He granted, reluctantly. "How's it going on the web?"

"Ok'ish. I'm in a group, we chat. It's mostly school and fashion."

"How old are you this week?"

"This week I'm mostly eleven. They're so easy. All desperate for 'friends'. How about you?"

"That stupid old man. Giving all that money to a drunk. Our money, Sis. Our money! I'm working on it. I think the best way to get at him is through his ex-wife. Did you see him in court! Useless twat." His voice deepened, a threat in it.

"I know where she is. Once we get these tags off, we'll go and get her. Do you remember the way she looked at us? Fucking snotty bitch. We'll have some fun with her before we *don't* give her back. Anyway, whatever, he'll cave in, and we'll get what's ours." He paused, then offered words of encouragement.

"Don't worry. Don't worry about people, don't worry about the system. I can fix all that. Don't worry about anything except us. It's all about us, nothing else." He stroked her arm.

"Have you found him yet?"

"Dear old Daddy? No. But I will. He can't hide forever but listen, I've had an idea."

She looked up. Getting used to his new face hadn't been easy. It was for their own good, they said. To protect them. His nose had sharpened, and his chin reduced. They didn't look like twins anymore and it was that more than anything else that she hated. She knew her own face wasn't the way she wanted it but did quite like the almond shape of her eyes and being a girl, she could have mad coloured hair. All those weeks looking through magazines at the models, trying to make choices. They'd been perfect as they were, just perfect. What had been done to them was wrong. Just plain wrong. She resented what had been forced on them.

"How about, once we've got the cash, we fuck off to America, get a motorhome and cruise. It's a big place and kids get lost all the time. We can have some fun. Like the old days."

"We can't drive." She said flatly, disappointed.

"We can learn and when we do, we can do whatever we like, wherever we like."

"Sounds like a plan." She said brightly, not entirely sure of how they'd overcome some of the more obvious issues like passports and driving licences, but she knew what Eddie was capable of. He could do anything on a computer.

"What about Mummy?"

"Fuck her. While we're at it we should think about ways of losing her. It can't be suicide though. I think that fucks up insurance claims. I'll have to check. But we need to get the money, all of it, hers, his and that pissed up fuckwit. Then we'll be free."

"You know best." She murmured.

Now he was on his back, she was stroking his tummy, getting closer. She could feel him stir. She giggled, looking up at him with her new cat's eyes, eyes he'd picked for her. She kept her gaze locked on him as she disappeared, her head slowly going under the sheet. Her voice was muffled as he heard her talking.

"Morning sleepy. Time to wake up. Mummy's here." He lay back, feeling the moistness of her mouth envelop him.

Devon

Sacha left Tom sleeping and went into the en suite. She thought about last night and the wisdom, or lack of it, that she'd shown. In the bright light of day though, she found a lightness in her mood. She'd known that the physical resurrection of their relationship had been inevitable. It had been within days of him turning up at the pub. Events since, shared experiences and the sense of togetherness that had developed folding back the intervening years. These past months with him had been cathartic and she could feel an end to the despair of the years since Ellen's death and knew that whatever it was she was going to feel when this was over, it wouldn't be the misery she'd lived with since that awful day. She'd deal with any new emotions as and when they surfaced, as she had last night.

It was Tom she was more concerned about. She could sense a fragility in him, that he was more likely to break than bend. She hoped that last night had strengthened him, had allowed more of the man he used to be to come through. She decided then, that she needed to build on last night, to keep him close. She needed him to regain some balance, restore his core beliefs not only in himself, but in her. Standing, she flushed and opened the bathroom door. She found Tom there, in the act of reaching for the handle.

She blushed slightly, lowering her eyes. "I'd give it five minutes if I were you."

He grinned. "I'll use the downstairs loo."

"Tom?"

He turned. "Yes?"

"You don't need to use the spare room anymore, not if you don't want to."

October. The Twins birthday came and went with no significant movement from the Prius. We wondered briefly if we'd tagged the right car, but our choice was verified by James and Ollie. *We've checked.*

As we sat out the next six weeks, while everyone else was ticking off the shopping days til Christmas, we were on a different kind of countdown, hopeful that we'd get something more tangible from the festivities than a pair of socks or perfume.

We carried on with our fitness programme and there were additional training sessions on such subjects as breaking and entering without actually doing any breaking. Lock picking, overcoming security systems and on one occasion, travelled to a country estate apparently owned and run by the Jedi.

The external security was impressive, and this particular estate had apparently been singled out as suitable as there was an old nuclear bunker on site. Going down into it revealed an extraordinarily large facility, stripped of its original fittings, it now contained a variety of scenarios. In full gear, we were taken through a 'house', picking out targets and live firing with our pistols. *You'd be surprised just how loud one of these things is when fired indoors. Get used to the flash, kick, noise, and smell of it all.*

Above ground, life went on as normal, the bunker utterly shutting out the mayhem taking place beneath.

The day before Christmas Eve, seated at his laptop James announced, "The Prius is out of London headed south-west." Christmas was temporarily forgotten as we watched its progress.

As it was the holiday season, and the weather not good, fog and rain, the traffic was horrendous. Stop, start, barely getting over 50mph. It was the best part of six hours later that he was satisfied the car had reached its destination.

"It's Devon. The middle of nowhere and hasn't moved for over an hour. Let's link the GPS to Google Earth."

We all hunched over the screen as he punched in co-ordinates, then zoomed in. We watched as Exeter appeared and then dropped south, the screen picking up more detail until the countryside became more lifelike. He settled at 1000ft above our target, studying the terrain.

"It's pretty much perfect." He moved back from the screen and pointed out the objects of his satisfaction with a finger.

"Can't tell yet but it looks like a farmhouse. We'll get closer in a minute. Firstly, it's set in a triangle bounded by hedgerows on all three sides. The road is south of the property and if I'm any judge, a 'B' road. The house itself is approached from the road by little more than a track and is set in the northern apex with the frontage facing southwest, down the hill if you like. Beyond that, to the north, more fields, more hedges. Nice and private. Nice and quiet. What works for them works equally well for us." He zoomed further in.

"Two outbuildings and the main house. Looks like they're traditional stone, perhaps been around for 200 years. Thatched roof." He zoomed in further, as close as Google could get then switched to street view, angling for the approach from eye level.

"Ok. You can see that from street view, the hedge bordering the road has a dry-stone wall in front of it which is about waist height." He moved the mouse left and right.

"There's a steel farm gate set into the wall to allow vehicle access." Unable to get an eye level view of the east and west hedgerows, he switched again to bird's eye and followed the property boundary from the gate, traversing left. Up, down and right until he was back at the gate again. He sat back.

"Ok. That's as much as we're gonna get from that. To recap. It's isolated, which is good. There's nothing but fields around it and as the main house is set in the top apex, you should be able to get close enough to scope it out without too much risk of being compromised. The next trick is to get you inserted."

James stood so Sacha and I shuffled closer to the laptop. She took the mouse and repeated the aerial reconnaissance. We were 99% certain that this was where the twins were holed up. In any event, we'd have to go and confirm what we believed.

James let us study for a while, aware that we now had something tangible to show for the past month's efforts and were savouring the moment. Then outlined what we'd be doing next.

"We need Mummy to leave before we do anything. The less footfall on site, the less chance of discovery.

So, we'll spend the next few days on the internet getting properly acquainted with the area and generally mooching. In the meanwhile, there is, of course, the small matter of Christmas to be celebrated. I need a volunteer to help me in the kitchen. Any takers?"

In the end, everyone mucked in. It was surreal. So much so, that I became introspective, wondering how life had changed. I didn't really remember Christmas much before Ellen had arrived and for the three years that she had been with us, well, it was a special time in our lives. After her last Christmas, there hadn't been much to celebrate. Sacha and I were living separate lives, and the drink and self-pity were as much as I could recall and was trying hard to forget, until now. Whether it was or not, for the time being at least, this felt like a new beginning, and I'd take it.

We were still sharing Sacha's room and the reconnection lent strength to my hopes for the future. The fact that we had a job to do gave us focus and I don't believe either of us really considered what would happen once events had taken their course. But having hope was something.

The Jedi were a tonic. They were constantly bouncing off each other and this spirit permeated throughout the house. Looking at them, listening to them, lifted us and lent an air of family to what was, by any standards, a strange scenario.

It was hard to believe that sitting around the table that lunchtime were three trained killers and a pair of divorcees with murder in mind. Gifts were exchanged, naturally we'd sourced some Star Wars stuff for The Jedi. In the same vein, from them, Sacha got a pampering kit, much needed if her hands were ever going to recover from the training, and I got a Pilgrims rugby shirt. *If you know, you know.* They said. *Don't wear it outside.*

Christmas over, we were assembled in the kitchen. The Jedi had loaded a flip chart onto an easel and Sid was standing by a table loaded with kit; clothing, binoculars, NVG's, sat phones, spare batteries, all stuff we were familiar with. Sacha and I were at the breakfast bar. Ollie spoke first.

"We're going to insert you next week, so the usual drill, please. Stop washing now, everything that goes in with you comes out with you. Clear?" We nodded in assent.

"It's going to be cold, especially at night so thermals, gloves, balaclavas. Sid's got all you need on the table. Between now and then, all your gear is either on you, or in your backpacks." He flipped the cover page of the chart to reveal an aerial map. One we were all familiar with.

"We've done some research and can tell you with some certainty that as we thought, this is where they are."

He extended an old car aerial and began highlighting out salient points on the map.

"The approach road. Only just wide enough for two careful cars to pass. We've identified a fixed passing point where the road widens briefly about 100 metres east of the house. That's where, in the early hours, we drop you. We'll rehearse the drop until it can be done swiftly and silently. From there, you go straight through the hedge and into the field. It was ploughed at the end of the season. Avoid treading on that area, tractors can only get so close to the edge of the field so there'll be a partly overgrown area you can use without leaving much in the way of footprints. Take your time." He was indicating our route with the pointer.

"Head west until you reach the corner of the property then north to the apex. From what we can see but without the benefit of a proper recce, you should be able to get within twenty metres of the main house without being skylined. From then on, get low and stay low. Be patient. When you're happy you have an unobstructed view of the frontage, get into the hedge, and settle in. You won't know how good your vantage point is until daylight. If you're exposed, try to eyeball a better position to move to but, if at all possible, stay where you are until nightfall.

Your best protection is to hunker down and keep still and quiet until you can move. They don't have a dog nor as far as we can tell, any livestock so unless they fancy doing a bit of gardening, which, in January, is highly unlikely, you should be ok. This is about identifying security systems, scoping out methods of entry, establishing the routine of the house. Nothing more. We give it a few days until you have the info we need then we extract. Clear?"

It was. We were apprehensive, but ready for this. Time to put into practice everything we'd learned. Grabbing our gear from Sid, we went upstairs to change. Most of it was the same kit we'd had all along, had trained in, some of it showing signs of wear but in good condition. As instructed, what we didn't put on, we packed into our rucksacks, pretty soon, it would take on the patina we were seeking.

It was a tough week, a period of waiting, studying, going over our routes, establishing comms routines and codewords. Should the Prius look like making an unscheduled comeback, that was 'The Broomstick'. The Twins were Bunny One and Bunny Two. We were Butch and Sundance. None of these should be needed, bur were in place if they were. Our extraction time was set for 3am, what night that would be would just be stated as 'tonight' and the extraction point was of necessity, where we'd been inserted.

The Jones Boys had a generic telecoms van. It was a 'ringer', in other words, there was a legitimate but identical van trundling somewhere around the system that they'd copied the number plates from. All the interior light bulbs had been removed and there was a flick switch in the front that would disable all exterior lights when we came to a stop. We were set.

They reckon practice makes perfect. Most of the route was motorway, only the last 45 minutes via minor routes. We'd left at 10pm and were approaching our drop off point in the dead of night, around 3am.

"Two minutes." Came the word from the front of the van.

We tugged our balaclava's down and faced each other. We'd been ready for over an hour but double checked anyway. Status, gear, appearance. It had been drilled into us and we weren't about to let ourselves or anyone else down by being dumb. I had my hand on the door latch and waited for the whispered word. We were so familiar with the lie of the road that we knew from its twists and turns where the drop off was. Feeling the van slow confirmed it.

"Go. Good Luck."

The latch clicked quietly, and oiled hinges swung open.

We hopped down and crouching, made for the hedge. The van slipped away, exhaust dissipating, tyre and engine noise fading, as we adjusted ourselves to our surroundings. The inside of the van had been pitch black and it took a minute or two to steady our breathing and to allow our eyes to adjust to the ambient light. There wasn't a lot of it but enough to make out edges and features. We needed to get to the other side of the hedge. It was strange but all our training made us feel more secure off the beaten track. We knew the hedge thinned a little just a few yards away. I reached for Sacha's hand and drew her face to mine.

"Ready?" I whispered. She nodded, and took the lead.

Carefully and quietly, we edged the few yards needed and negotiating a minor drainage ditch, got on our bellies and shrugged our way into the field. Still tense but feeling easier out of sight of the road, we knew where we were heading and wordlessly followed the hedgeline first west, then, at the junction, north. It was only about 600 yards to where we hoped our lying up point would be. Getting closer to the apex of the field, we could see no lights from the house, its occupants either out or sleeping. We had no way of knowing which.

We crept into the dense cover offered by the base of the hedge. With luck, come morning, this would be our home for the next couple of days and nights. No words were needed.

Silently, sleeping bags were unrolled and crawled into, and essential kit put to hand. It was freezing, something I'd noticed but disregarded en route. Now we were still, it came to the fore. We'd take an hour to sort ourselves out, scrape away hip hollows in the dirt, trim any low hanging stems that might whip, generally secure ourselves. Then we'd set the watch, Sacha taking first stint.

I felt a gentle nudge and surfaced from within the sleeping bag, just my eyes at first, keeping the cloud from my breath inside the bag until I could cover my mouth with a scarf. It was hard to tell precisely what time it was, mist obscured the area and whatever moonlight there was, offered little by way of a clue. I checked my watch. 6am. Quietly, as per our training, we got our faces as close to each other as we could and in muffled voices considered our position.

We were about thirty metres from the main house and while we could see it quite clearly, we were happy that unless someone walked right on top of us, we were secure. Tucked inside the cover of the hedge, there were no surprises on either side or behind us. All in all, we felt happy that there would be no need to move. In an ideal world, there would have been two teams, one covering the front, the other out back. But this wasn't combat. We were here to observe, and our enemy was unlikely to be battle aware.

Their main concern was staying put and keeping a low profile. We figured their mindset wouldn't include a rural observation post as a possibility, let alone a threat. As long as we kept still and quiet and didn't do anything stupid that might expose us, with time, we would get the information we needed. 100% confirmation they were there, that they were alone and that there was a way to get to them. Sacha hunkered down in her sleeping bag as I took the next watch.

Early risers they weren't. The mist had cleared hours ago, and a low sun had risen behind us. I was wide awake and had let Sacha sleep on. Days and nights of doing this exact same thing in our own back yard had shown me my limits and abilities and I knew that after a couple of hours shuteye, I'd be good for the first day before getting into the routine proper. We had prearranged signals with the Jedi that just needed a thumb to send. I picked up the sat phone, hit the preset, let it ring three times and switched it off. *All ok fellas. No need to move.*

Lights came on in the house. Reaching over, I guessed where Sacha's shoulder was and squeezed once. It was second nature for us both. I felt her stir beneath my hand then released my grip. Slowly, she came up for air, eyes blinking, silently aware. I jerked my head towards the house, a movement consisting only of millimetres. It happened suddenly. One minute we hadn't clapped eyes on these little shits for years, the next, there was one of them, in plain sight.

Eddie, using a side door, putting out the trash, having a little yawn and a stretch, scratching his ass, taking his time, as normal as you like. I felt Sacha tense beside me and a rush of adrenalin of my own. I shoved it down and simultaneously became aware that Sacha had also relaxed. We'd been warned what to expect and how to react. There was no room for instinct here. Everything had to be clinical. They were just targets, nothing more. Remembering the end game and the fact that it was possible, made it a simple thing not to rush out from our hiding place and club the little fucker. I reached for the bino's. Saw what I needed to see then passed them to Sacha. Eddie ambled back inside. Sacha rested the bino's and looked me straight in the eye. Her look was fearsome but controlled, then triumphant. Through gritted, tense teeth she whispered, "Got them."

My eyes and face, reflected, said the same thing. *Oh, yes. We've got them alright.*

They spent much of the time in the house. That worked for us on one level but not too well on others. We had a thirst to see more of them. Glimpses of Eddie and Verity in the great outdoors weren't enough. We had to get closer. Sniff around their lives and root out how to get at them.

We spent three days and nights there all told. Watching. Studying.

We got used to their presence. It was a bit like having to pick up a scorpion. Fear and unfamiliarity giving way to the examination process.

Adolescence had given way to adulthood and the years had been kind to them. They were, it had to be said, handsome specimens. Hair colour and style had been changed but that was to be expected and they had clearly had some plastic surgery. Subtle differences but sufficient so that they were no longer identical. I'm guessing that as minor as they were, it would have been something of a sacrifice to abandon their once unique appearance. Eddie appeared to be scraping around the 6ft mark and looked like he worked out. That meant he was likely to be a handful if it all got up close and personal. In her own way, I reckon Sacha had sized up Verity and measured her chances. If those two ended up fighting us for their lives, we had a problem.

They never went out together, at least not while we were there. If errands had to be run, it was Verity that did the running, mostly though, stuff was delivered. Groceries left in a secure bin obviously set there for that purpose. The delivery guy had a key and would open the bin, drop the stuff in and lock it behind him. Only then would one of them shuffle out and repeat the process in reverse, always with an eye on the driveway.

It was on the third night that we decided to risk approaching the house. Where we were was all well and good for scoping out security, access, the rhythm of the house, but told us nothing of what went on inside and it was that information that was needed. The decision made, we got our gear together, sent the Jedi a message that we'd be extracting in the early hours and readied ourselves.

We knew their routine. During the day, not much clue as to what they were doing, their comings and goings only hinted at but becoming more evident at night. At dusk, lights would go on in what was apparently the living room, bedtime though, was erratic, indicated by stair lights going on and off and the illumination of one upstairs bedroom. Sacha and I eyeballed each other at that confirmation of our suspicions. They had to be fucking each other. We'd decided that 9pm would be the optimum time to leave our hide and get closer but it was a little earlier, around 8.45 that the lighting downstairs suddenly changed. The curtains obscured any detail but leaking through them we got the impression that some kind of disco was taking place, flashing lights of varying hues, colour and intensity emanating from the living room. It made no difference. If anything, if there was a party, it'd mean less chance of discovery.

We let things get into full swing and at 9pm, moved out, towards the house.

The bulky gear we had no choice other than to leave behind in the hope that we'd be able to retrieve it. If we were cautious, it shouldn't be a problem and we had every intention of being ultra-careful. We knew where the security lights were and that they were movement activated. We'd seen them set off by foxes trying to get at the trash. This was a regular occurrence and The Twins had grown complacent. Unless there was a sharp noise accompanying the light, they ignored it, just a twitching curtain any hint that they were concerned. If we had to, we'd set them off then get under them, below the living room windowsill. Leave it a minute, then hope for a crack in the curtains, try to get a look inside.

Everything the Jedi taught us came into play. If you needed to focus on an object in the dark, look off a degree or two and let it come into view, then zone in. If you needed to isolate a noise, look in its direction with your mouth open, at night, in otherwise complete silence, it amplifies and can be sourced. We covered the thirty metres undetected, noiseless. The security light came on as expected and we rolled underneath it, up against the wall, waiting. No one took any notice.

When we got our eyes level with the living room window, through a chink in the curtains, we could see why. There was a trapeze like set up, or at least in our initial surprise, that was our first thought. But it wasn't.

It was more, much more than that. There were two separate arrangements, one for each player, both having dozens of ropes of varying thickness and lengths, not all of which were in use. They were coiled around their bodies, some under tension, some not, suspending them some three feet from the floor. Aside from something strapped to an ankle, probably an electronic tag, they were both naked. Blindfolded, Verity was suspended in a cradle made entirely of rope, elements of which snaked out to create loops which bound her hands behind her. Belly down, back arched, she was incapable of independent movement, her brother lending her volition and direction as he passed by in his own elaborate setup, touching and stroking as he did so.

If we hadn't known they were brother and sister, it might not have been so weird. Strange for sure, but watching what they were doing to each other, how and where his fingers and mouth touched and lingered and her reaction to it, it was obscene. The ropes were an expensive, pure white, suspended from a marionette like control fixed to solid ceiling beams. Choreographed, practised, they were rapt. It was all we needed to see. There was nothing to be gained from pure voyeurism but still, it was tough to tear your eyes away, so subdued and controlled was the lighting on what in other circumstances, would have been a bewitching aerial ballet.

As I took a last look around, my gaze was drawn to the back of the room, to the hearth. Above it was a projected image. Through the haze and confusion of the lighting, I couldn't quite focus on the image that was there, small beams of light flashing across it, sometimes whiting it out. I concentrated a little harder, trying to zone in. I wish I hadn't. My subconscious tried to warn me, the hair on the back of my neck rising, my face flushing with a thousand red pinpricks but my eyes didn't get the message in time and stayed riveted to the screen.

It was Ellen. Our Ellen. Standing alone, one mitten missing, and it was that tiny detail that made me realise exactly what I was watching. She had a confused look about her, uncertain, a little afraid, then, Verity came into shot. She crouched behind Ellen, her hands on her shoulders, pointing towards the camera, smiling. Then, her expression changed, her eyes narrowing, her smile slowly receding until it became a gin trap full of malice. Pulling her arm back to its fullest extent, she clenched her right hand and let go with a fist that caught Ellen in the back of the head. The last image I had before my main fusebox tripped, was Ellen's face as she went down hard, her mouth in a big, round, 'O' of surprise and pain. As I slumped, my back to the wall, I felt the touch of The Horseman, saw the gleam in his eye, his raised sword and began to disintegrate, to fail.

Beside her, Sacha had sensed a change in Tom, felt him go rigid. Following his horrified, wide-eyed gaze, she found the cause, recognising the sick flick instantly. The back of her mind registered surprise, shock, and a burning anger that somehow, it was still out there. But she'd seen it a million times, years of sleepless nights, of transforming her notion of what she'd first seen in Court from horror to disgust helped her now and she shovelled those images into a dark, narrow crevice in her head, and pulling herself away, she switched her attention to Tom.

His eyes were blank, expressionless, his arms wrapped around his knees, almost in the foetal position. She had to get him back, but not yet. Provided he was quiet, motionless, she needed him to stay that way. She put a hand on his shoulder, there was no response, so she let it stay there as a means of detecting change then, raised her head and looked back into the room. With an effort of will she ignored the screen and studied the tableau in front of her. Taking it in, committing it to memory, was the work of only a minute or so. Time to go. Beneath her hand, Tom had remained motionless, she bent down and put her face close to his, her hand now gripping his jaw.

From somewhere way off in the distance, I felt hands on my face, lifting it, gripping me hard, demanding attention.

The discomfort deflected me and somehow, I cracked open my mind and saw that Sacha was out there, was searching for me. This was unfamiliar territory. Before, whenever The Horseman came, it was just me and him. No comfort, no friends other than booze and oblivion. Hope bubbled up tentatively, and though fearful of what might lay in wait, I ventured out to join her.

Every feature of her face, the set of her mouth, the fierce light in her eyes said, *Don't you dare! Not now!* I stopped falling as The Horseman retreated. The sparks fizzing in my brain subsided and some of my lights came back on. I nodded once, the movement dislodging tears. Grabbing my hand, she tugged, jerking me away from the wall. Almost catatonic, I copied her every move and somehow that got me back to the hide.

Back in the hide, I could think of only one thing. "They still have her."

The words fell from me, choked, strangled. Sacha put a finger to her lips, quietening me and with kind, understanding eyes whispered, "Not now."

I spent the next five hours fighting back, Sacha the only thing standing between me and my nemesis.

Extraction was at 3am. During the wait, Sacha kept one hand on me. A hard one, flat on my chest, either holding me down or as reassurance, I couldn't say. The rest of her attention stayed focussed on the house. The house where in my mind, Ellen's murder was happening, being savoured. Lips were being licked and sick minds aroused. Waiting for pick-up was the longest night of my life. I had nowhere to go, no bottle to crawl into, no pills promising unconsciousness. Five eons where an image I'd avoided all these years became a detail engraved in my brain. There wasn't a box on earth that would ever contain it but there was someone with me now.

That night. I sucked it up. Pushed back where before surrender had been the easy option. We'd suffered independently, unnecessarily, hadn't communicated. Didn't understand, not the murder, and since then, not each other. But that wasn't true anymore, and I drew fortitude from Sacha's suffering. I wasn't alone with this. Because we'd shared, I now had someone to help me find a way through the guilt and back out into a free space. It didn't matter that the catalyst for this epiphany was our shared objective of the past few months, nor did I care overmuch about the years of self-pity. They might not have been such a waste. After all, without them, how could I have known the difference between then and now.

But the fall had been so gradual and so full of events, the trial, conviction, being part of all that had gone on but so desperate not to be, that I hadn't realised my counsellor had been there all the time. That if I'd simply asked, communicated, then a lot of needless suffering could and should have been avoided.

I wondered at length about how much of a part I could have played in Sacha's healing process and realised that there was more to loving someone than simply saying the words, believing them and having them believed. This and more went through my mind as the picture of Ellen going down played over and over again on a constant loop but slowly, ever so slowly, being with Sacha, having her there and knowing that she'd sat through the entire tape with a quiet courage made me feel something more than the deep melancholy that had suffused my life. I felt ashamed. No-one should have had to go through that alone and because of me, the one person I cared about more than myself had been forced to do just that.

The pickup was done wordlessly, as rehearsed, a simple thumbs up from Sacha as she bundled me and our gear into the van. The journey home was undertaken in silence. Sacha sat with her back to the bulkhead, me resting against her, her arms wrapped around me, holding me, and helping me hold on as my head reset itself. Her words helped as she stroked my hair and whispered, *I've got you, Tom. I've got you.* Somehow, I slept.

I was woken by the van doors opening. We hadn't moved. Sacha still held me, and I knew, I just knew she would have stayed there doing just that, for as long as it took. What I'd seen, what I'd tried desperately all these years to avoid, while temporarily unmanning me, was now nothing to fear. It had happened. She was dead. Let the why and how go. Remember her for what she was and the simple joy that came with her, honour her memory. And while the future might see me falter, I knew now a way back existed.

I was ashamed of how spineless, how useless, how worthless I'd been. How I'd abandoned my best friend to carry the weight of the manner of our baby's death. I would use that shame. I'd cope somehow. I set my face straight and turned to the mother of my child.

"I'm ok. Thank you."

Sacha searched my expression, studied my tone. "Are you back?"

I took her by the shoulders and looked her straight in the eye. "I have a way now. I may still be haunted but the ghosts don't frighten me anymore. Do you believe me?"

She looked at me again. I don't know if the way I felt manifested itself as anything tangible, something detectable, but I did know it was there and hoped she might see it.

Sacha relaxed visibly and her eyes softened. "I'm glad."

"Good." I said, grabbing our gear and making for the door. "Come on. We have things to do." We clambered from the van and made our way into the house.

Sid had a hot meal and a brew on the go. Deep in thought, we ate and drank. Sacha seemed on edge, itching to get away from the table.

"Guys. I know we need to debrief but there's something I've gotta do. It's important. I need an hour."

She looked around the room, as if asking permission to duck.

"Something to do with last night?" I asked.

She nodded. "Tell them what you saw."

"Do you mind, fellas?" I asked. "I can go through the house routine and security setup. And there's been a development."

I was going to get through that in a business-like fashion. Anything else would be a backward step.

The Jedi nodded; their curiosity piqued. Sacha left quickly. In her absence, using the flip chart and diagrams we'd made during the op, I ran through any changes that had occurred and corrected the photos. Security dealt with; I dropped two bombshells.

"They still have the footage they shot of Ellen."

"What foo...? Then Ollie got it. A moment's silence then "How?"

I'd been thinking about this and there could really only be one explanation.

"It was in evidence during the trial. Evidence that must, by law, be shared with the defence."

"So you're saying...?"

"Mummy. Fucking Mummy. It seems she doesn't just defend them. She feeds their needs. She has to have made a copy."

"Twisted cow."

"Twisted, warped? Don't know, don't fucking care. We'll deal with her later. There's more"

I told them about the tableau, the lights, ropes, music, and the dance. I'd just finished raising their eyebrows when Sacha came back into the room.

"Ok. I'm guessing Tom has filled you in on their Indian Rope Trick?"

Sacha had a sheaf of printouts in one hand and a coffee in the other.

Like Tom, she was still in her ops gear, going to Devon had answered some questions but more than that, had created new possibilities. Ideas she was keen to explore. She'd taken that extra minute, when Tom was catatonic, to look very hard at what was in front of her. Without waiting for any meaningful response, she continued.

"Except it 'aint Indian. It's Japanese."

Pausing to distribute printouts harvested from the internet, she moved over to the flip chart. She wasn't intending to use it but as this was where briefings were delivered, it was the focal point of the room.

"Shibari. To be precise, or at least, some perversion of it. It's literal meaning is, 'to tie', but over the years, it's been experimented with as an erotic practice. These two appear to have based what they're doing only on the elements of it that suit them. What you have there are pictures of the more traditional form, just to illustrate the basics. Ten minutes on the internet was all it took to find those but I'm guessing deeper research will give us a better idea of how best to use this."

Tom stood and joined her; he'd clicked onto where she was going with this.

"We've never been really comfortable with the idea of shooting anyone, not even them. You probably know that there was a time when being caught wasn't an issue, at least in the beginning, when it was just me. That's changed and gunshot wounds aren't an option anymore. It's too obviously a murder and a high profile one at that, which will force an in-depth investigation. We'll be looked at."

Sacha took up the narrative.

"Everything that they did to Ellen had just one aim. Pleasure. We all know about this weird bond, this weird communion they're supposed to share, and we think it's time they got the ultimate high."

"This," she continued, "gives us an opening. If we can catch them at it, suspended, wrapped up, call it what you will, they'll be vulnerable. All we'll need the guns for is control, what we need to figure out is how to make this spooky shit work for us and against them, accidents can happen, we want to be there to see that one does." She paused to let the possibilities form.

"A bit of history first." She fingered back a loose lock of hair and looked down at her notes.

"Its origins lie in martial arts, in this case, Hojo-jutsu, which was a means of restraining prisoners used in Japan for about 300 years from 1400 or so.

Yeah, I know. I'd never heard of it either. Basically, a Samurai thing. The more sophisticated the technique was, the more honour they were showing their prisoner, according to rank. A century or so later, it evolved into Kinbaku, erotic bondage. Nowadays though, it's classed as a kind of erotic spirituality and as I said, generally referred to as Shibari, a country mile from the original martial art and is a game for two, a rigger and the model, but because of the way these two have messed with it the game has changed. This is where it gets complicated, and I've only had a few minutes with this so bear with me."

She paused, thoughtful, concentrating. Tom took this as a cue to re-join the Jedi. Sacha looked up from her printout.

"Right. In its original form, the idea was to use the ropes to create patterns and shapes that either contrast with or complement the natural curves of the human body. Master riggers know where and how to position knots to stimulate pressure points to enhance the model's experience but there's something else that can be achieved and that's where I figure these two are getting their buzz from." Sacha paused, studying her notes to be sure she got it right.

"There's a belief that Shibari can stimulate Ki energy flow and transfer, Ki being an unseen life force, a universal energy that penetrates everywhere.

That it increases levels of endorphins and other hormones and creates a trance like experience for the model and an adrenaline rush for the rigger. It's called, 'Rope Drunk'. From what we witnessed, we know they also use sound and light to amplify the experience but here's the thing, if their affinity really does stretch as far as bouncing physical highs off each other, imagine all those chemicals flowing back and forth, magnifying, there's a power exchange going on and when it happens, my bet is that those two will be in another world."

As that idea flowed around the room, James used the moment to ask, "But they both wear the ropes simultaneously, from what you saw, have you worked out how they got into position or more importantly, how it all ends, and they disengage?"

"No. To be honest, we were knocked back by what they were doing and were too surprised, shocked, if you like, to take it all in."

Tom stood. "We know the indicators. The Northern lights erupting in the living room means it's playtime. We need to see what goes on, from start to finish. That's why we must go back."

There was a general agreement in the room that not going back wasn't an option.

"Fair enough." Said Ollie. "It's been a long few days. Let's take some time out and look at the weather for next week. In the meantime, we'll have a few practice sessions at knot tying and generally getting you two used to rope handling. Those two weird fuckers aside, knots are an art form. For now, you two stink. Sort yourselves out and get some kip. There's stuff me 'n Jimbob need to organise."

"Before you do that, I have a question."

Ollie and James looked at Tom.

"We noticed they were wearing what we reckon are electronic tags."

"And?" Queried James.

"Did you know about that? If they're tagged, I reckon you two could easily have hacked into the system and told us exactly where they were all the time. London and tagging Mummy wouldn't have been necessary. Also, you've hinted all along that they were probably in a rural location. But you knew that, didn't you?"

James sighed, looked at Ollie, who nodded, then answered slowly. "Whether we did or not, whether we could have or not, is academic."

James paused briefly, sensing that Tom and Sacha felt aggrieved, of having been left out of the loop, then continued in a placatory tone.

"Guys. This isn't about what we can or can't do, what we do or don't know. It's about you. How you need to learn and adapt your thinking if you really want to do this. Otherwise, why not simply give us a million apiece and have us do it for you? And what would you get from that? Trust me…trust us. It needs to be this way. We know."

Tom and Sacha looked at each other. They'd never wanted to think ill of the Jedi and there was an understanding now that some things they simply weren't going to be told. Things they'd have to work out and do for themselves if they wanted the kind of closure that money couldn't buy. The atmosphere in the room changed from a mild resentment to recognition and acceptance, the meeting breaking up with a return to business.

The forecast for early next week was fair. Cold but not much rain expected, certainly no hint of snow. Resting, recuperating, was interspersed with the promised knot tying lessons. Hitches, bends, sheets, bowlines, all studied and practised until they could be performed quickly and easily. Sacha's favourite was the self-tightening half hitch.

A simple knot that could easily occur accidentally around two moving objects. She practised while wearing gloves. Based on what Sacha had seen, James and Ollie recreated the roping set up. They weren't identical. The one used by Eddie had a series of pulleys and carabiners not visible on Verity's set up. Further research showed that this meant Eddie was a 'self-rigger.' In other words, having set Verity up in her arrangement, he could self-tie and then raise himself into position and tie off. They were ignoring every safety rule in the book, but it seemed that their mutual pleasure meant more to them than taking basic precautions. Tom was more interested in the arousal process, this so called 'Rope Drunk'. An idea had formed that was beginning to take on shape.

Ropework

They were back in Devon. The insertion had been trouble free and nothing had changed. Nothing except that the nearby fields, including one they had to circuit, had been treated with slurry. The stench clung to them instantly. Having opted not to revisit their first observation post, and confident that The Twins felt secure, their chosen location was south of the original but about 10 meters closer. Settling in, they waited.

It was the on second night that the lights started. Making a note of the time, they nodded to each other, then silently left the hide, and made their way over to the living room window. As before, the security light flicked on as they approached and again, they passed swiftly beneath it and reached the wall of the house. They gave it a minute or so before raising their eyes level with the windowsill. The scene was pretty much as before. Tom's peripheral vision told him there was a screen above the hearth, a detail he compartmentalised while taking in everything else. Verity was already in position, hog tied, naked, blind, and waiting. Eddie had set himself up and using his pulley arrangement, was elevating himself to her level.

They watched as he tied off, securing the free end of the pulley rope to a cleat. He let go and swung gently towards his sister, giving her a gentle push as he drifted past. Clearly practised, they began their dance. Neither Tom nor Sacha absorbed the erotic detail, instead they studied facial expression, how the ropes moved around on their moorings, twists that Eddie initiated to gain centrifugal force, spinning them out like sky divers as the ropes untwisted. He was adept and knew how to lose and gain momentum or direction, what to do when their bodies touched, knowing what his sister anticipated and was eager for. If it hadn't been them, it might have been art, but this was repellent and sickening but Tom and Sacha stuck to the task, studying the detail only to bring an end to anything and everything they represented.

The music and lights, muted at first, began to build as Eddie drew closer, spent more time entwined, hugging, caressing, breaking off, a gentle tug bringing them back into the clinch. During this phase, whatever they'd built up between them was clearly reaching its climax. Sweating, intent on his sister, Eddie's urgent fingers found pressure points and erogenous zones. Stroking, always stroking until the moment when the music reached its loudest and the lights coalesced and homed in on the junction of their bodies.

Eddie grabbed his sister and mirrored her bound pose, glistening limbs stretched, backs arched, and heads were thrown back, mouths open, panting with ecstasy, the perfect image of a Rorschach test as the lights went out and the music ceased suddenly. For a minute or two, they remained suspended, stroking, and nuzzling as their passion diminished then Eddie released his sister and reached for the cleated end of the rope. His damp skin highlighted the muscles beneath which rippled, illustrating the effort needed to stay in position whilst freeing himself. Undone, he slowly paid out the line and the pulleys did the rest.

On the floor, he slid from his bonds and stood, free of any tie. Taking off her blindfold he then took a few minutes to carefully release his sister until she too was free. They stood in the centre of the room, beneath a single blue spotlight and held each other. Tired but not quite done, they moved to the sofa and sitting side by side, legs open and hands busy, they brought themselves to another climax. Caressing, stroking still, they lay down together and slid into a satiated doze.

Tom and Sacha, busy as they were writing notes, had ignored each other during this display but now it was over, turned silently and their eyes met. Some situations don't need words, just an expression and this one was acknowledged with raised eyebrows and a release of air, as if they'd been holding their breath.

They crept silently back to the hide and got ready for extraction.

Tom stood by the flip chart. Their notes now collated and writ large. "That's it. From start to finish. Eddie's the rigger, as we guessed and the whole thing, including the sofa business, takes them about half an hour."

Ollie and James had sat silently until now. James raised the question. "And you're sure this is the way it goes. Every time?"

"Fairly sure. The first time we saw this they were about ten minutes in and that tallies with last night. Also, the music and lights were the same as before. It's all timed. We reckon they've found their niche and it's repetitive, rehearsed, all about anticipation."

"So, we know what they do and how long it takes. When do you figure to interrupt?"

Tom turned to Ollie. "When they get to the vinegar stroke and have no control, but we need to be inside when that happens, ready to bounce them."

The floorplan of the Devon house was straightforward. Tom reckoned that the exterior kitchen door was the easiest lock to crack and once inside, it was only a few yards to the doorway out of the kitchen and into a small hallway which was the hub of the ground floor. Access to the living room was straight off it. The Jedi set up practice doors with an identical set up to the farmhouse. From their recce, Tom had established that it was fitted with a nightlatch that was operated by a lever inside and a key from the exterior. Tom could crack it in less than 30 seconds and in virtual silence.

"Now for the tricky bit." James announced. They were in the kitchen studying the ropes suspended from the ceiling.

"We know we can rely on Eddie to secure Verity before tying himself off, so his ropes are the ones we need to study. A volunteer is worth ten pressed men so Ollie, if you don't mind?" James used both hands, like a magician presenting an illusion, to invite Ollie to step up.

"I knew it was going to be me." Ollie said fatalistically, getting to his feet and ambling over.

Even with their notes it took a while to get it just right but eventually, Ollie was in suspension, neatly trussed but clearly unhappy.

"Now what?" He grunted.

"OK." Said James. "We know that Verity has a similar set up but is basically unable to move her hands. We need to figure out a way of ensuring Eddie is similarly indisposed, so let's get to it."

With prompting from Ollie, using free hanging lines and some discussion, a method was established that did the trick without over complication.

"The only criteria is that this needs to look like an accident. Eddie, being the rigger, must be in a situation where he's in a tangle and can't help his sister. Between the two of them, because they've ignored basic safety rules, it doesn't look too difficult but you two can't leave a mark on them. No evidence. Are you happy you can achieve that?"

Sacha and Tom nodded. All the ropework they'd been doing had culminated here in the dress rehearsal had left them confident that they at least had the ability to immobilise The Twins. What came after that couldn't be rehearsed, not the way they'd do it nor the way they might feel once it was done.

"Can I get down now?"

They were in. For the third and hopefully last time the insertion had gone quietly and efficiently.

All they had to do now was hunker down and wait for the light show. The next four days and nights were cold one's. The rain didn't help constantly dripping from the leaves and stems that hid them. They were wet and uncomfortable but that didn't matter. There was a tension and sense of anticipation that shut out everything but their observation.

On the fourth night, at 8.45pm, the lights inside the house began to flicker against the curtains. It was showtime. Tom and Sacha knew what was going on inside the house but still, they had to be sure. Sacha crouched beneath the window while Tom, waiting for her signal, was at the kitchen door. They were connected by a length of twine. He felt three hard tugs. Working on the lock he felt it give at the sweet spot. He tugged back on the line and momentarily, Sacha joined him, bundling the twine as she came. Once she was at his back, he gently pushed against the door. It creaked slowly open.

The music level, no longer contained by the house, was an acoustic thud that hit them at the same as the warmth inside. Tom took out his gun, it was already cocked, it had been for the last 96 hours. All it needed was a finger on the trigger, his hovered, ready. On their haunches, they went in, alert, looking for kitchen like obstacles, vegetable racks, rubbish bins any kind of trip hazard that might betray their presence.

Quietly, still crouched low, Sacha closed the door behind her with a gentle click. The door to the hallway was open and seeing it as an invitation, they half stood and on tiptoe, made their way over to the frame. Nothing had changed. There was no sense of anything out of the ordinary, no shouts could be heard, and the music and lights remained constant. So far so good.

The hallway was carpeted. A pleasant surprise that dulled their approach to the living room. Tom reached behind him and found Sacha's arm. He gave her a gentle squeeze of reassurance, something he didn't quite feel himself. He heard the soft scrape of metal on canvas and knew Sacha now had her gun in her hand. They were ready. The waited until the music reached its crescendo, the signal for the Rorschach moment and as the last drumbeat echoed around the house, Tom pushed open the door, striding in with Sacha right behind him.

He was aware that as before, Ellen might feature on the screen. He had accepted that as a reality and was as ready as he could be to face it. Nevertheless, the tug was irresistible. One quick glance confirmed her presence. This time though, she was as the Police had found her, face down in the mud. She was being circled, the camera moving around her body. The skin over his cheekbones tightened and momentarily, he was unable to breathe.

Remembering where he was and what he was here to do, he pulled his eyes away and scanned to where he knew Eddie and Verity would be. There they were, as seen before but this time there was an aroma, the scent of sex and exertion that lent a new dimension to the canvas. It took a moment for Eddie to realise they weren't alone anymore. A moment where Tom and Sacha got into position, taking a twin each, but out of arms reach. Guns levelled, the temptation was to shoot them there and then. Neither Tom nor Sacha had any intention of engaging with The Twins. This was a job. Theirs to do with no fucking about.

The Twins awareness occurred simultaneously. Shock and surprise mixed with the rapturous high they'd just achieved. Their faces reflected the moment when their dream turned into a nightmare, from flushed pink by exertion and ecstasy, to pale as blood drained away and endorphins were replaced by fear inspired adrenalin.

Eddie shouted. "What the fuck!"

Still wearing her blindfold and unable to see, Verity's head jerked left and right, trying to sense what was happening. Eddie reacted by instinctively pulling himself over to the cleat.

Tom got there first, striding across the room and stamping his foot hard on the free end of the rope coil, preventing its release.

For the hell of it, he thrust his gun in Eddie's face. It loomed large, too large for Eddie to focus on but some kind of awareness must have kicked in and he immediately released his hold on the tethering rope, swinging gently back towards his sister. Bumping into her, he adjusted and then for the first time centred on what Tom was holding. There was the immediate and strong stench of shit in the room.

"Eddie! What is it! What's going on?" Verity's voice was shrill, piercing the air.

Silence reigned momentarily as The Twins tried to acclimatise to their new environment. Tom knew that this was the moment when he was supposed to just bag Eddie, but the image of Ellen took over.

"Shit yourself, have you Eddie? Thinking about fight or flight? Seems to me you only have the one option and you've exercised it."

"Who's that! Eddie!" Blinded and confused, Verity was panicking.

Eddie reddened and twisted against the now soiled ropes that held him aloft. It was futile and he knew it, the only way out of his rig was the cleat behind the man in black. The man with a gun. Beside him his sister set up a whimpering background noise.

Her head had drooped, denying reality. Beside her, Tom saw Sacha who like him, had yet to do what had been agreed.

"What do you want." His voice was an octave higher than he intended and made a concentrated effort to lower it. "Who are you? Take what you want and fuck off. We haven't got any cash."

"This isn't about money." Eddie turned his head, confused at the sound of a woman's voice.

Sacha tugged her balaclava off. Shaking her hair out, she raised her head and looked the tethered youth smack in the eye. It took a while to see beyond the threat of the gun and images of people dressed in black then confusion was replaced by comprehension, and it shattered what was left of his grasp of events.

Verity was struggling against her bonds, still ignorant of what was going on around her, she was intent only on getting free, wriggling from side to side and trying to loosen the ropes that bound her hands. Sacha steadied the top rope and once the struggle had subsided stooped to eye level and lifting Verity's blindfold said, "Remember me?"

Recoiling at the sudden, unexpected touch, Verity blinked against the light, then recognising the stranger, it clicked.

"We didn't mean it!" She shrieked. "It was an accident! That's what everyone said!"

Sacha looked towards Tom and having caught his gaze, flicked her eyes towards the screen over the hearth. Tom nodded. Together, they manoeuvred The Twins to a position where they had no choice other than to view the screen.

"Does that look like an accident to you?" Sacha's voice had taken on a timbre Tom hadn't heard before.

"She's the only reason we're here. If you'd left our family alone, none of this would be happening. You could have carried on fiddling with each other, and no-one would be any the wiser. Now though, this is how you'll be found."

"Found! What do you mean, found? What are you going to do?" Eddie's voice had cracked.

Tom held the gun level with the side of Eddie's head, just out of arm's reach. Sacha released her hold on Verity, who, still immobilised, spun slowly clockwise back to centre. Stepping towards Eddie, Sacha took one of the many spare lines hanging from the rig.

"Hands behind your back. There's a good boy." Said Tom, flicking the gun for emphasis.

"What are you going to do!" Eddie's voice was back up there, shrill in alarm. He resisted, but once Sacha had secured one hand, the other soon followed.

Eddie squirmed his head sideways, trying to see what Sacha was doing. Trying to stop this from happening. But she'd practised. Rehearsed. In less than a minute Eddie was trussed and going nowhere. Moving over to a small table, Sacha took out a mobile phone.

"You know what this is, don't you?"

She propped it up against a table lamp and sighting it, selected video and switched it on.

Verity started to scream. "You bitch! You fucking bitch!" Tears came, then hysterics. Eddie was shouting, spitting, and foaming at the mouth, wriggling, desperate to break free.

"We didn't mean it!" Tom didn't register which one had screamed that last denial, just that it was we, always, we.

Sacha stepped back to Verity and taking a clear, plastic bag from her pocket, she saw Tom do the same. Inside them were identical bags. Identical but sterile, no clothing fibres, no DNA. Tom and Sacha looked at one another. It was almost as if a sigh passed between them then, as practised, they simply slid the bags over The Twin's heads.

Tom had read all about erotic asphyxiation. How accidents happen. The basic premise was that by reducing the flow of oxygen through the carotid artery during sex, the ultimate high could be achieved. The trick was to get the bag off before suffocation occurred. Or, depending on the desired outcome, to leave it on until it did.

Tom stood rock still, braced, the plastic bag bunched tight in his right hand, behind the nape of Eddie's neck. A sweet spot. The Twins squirmed. Eddie's muscles bunched as he struggled to break free, sweat streaming from his pores, making him slippery beneath Tom's gloves. The ropes creaked, tightening, and loosening with every movement, movements that grew weaker as the seconds slipped away.

The average, untrained human being can hold their breath for about 30 or 40 seconds. Tom could see Sacha having a slightly easier time with Verity. Her face was grim. Unforgiving. Tom had an idea his was set the same. Abstractedly, Tom noted that his heartbeat wasn't raised…if anything it had slowed to about 60 beats a minute. His muscles dealt with Eddie; his mind was somewhere else.

From within, inside his head, he heard a dull rap, but couldn't quite figure out where it was coming from. He heard it again, polite but quite insistent.

Concentrating hard, his focus was drawn to a corner of his mind that had been kept shut tight. A dark place. The Toybox. There was someone inside trying to get out. Not trapped though, not this time, just ready to leave. He felt ok gently releasing the latch and allowing the lid to open. A small hand appeared on the rim and quietly, softly, Ellen clambered out. She was in her nightclothes, Teddy hanging from her right hand. Her face was pink and scrubbed, her hair brushed, shiny and knot free. She looked nothing like the torn and battered image being played out over the hearth. She smiled.

Hello, Daddy.

Hello Sweetheart.

I think I can go to sleep now.

He nodded. Ok, sweetheart. Whatever you say.

Goodnight, Daddy.

Goodnight, baby girl.

She, Teddy and the Toybox faded. Not quite disappearing but receding to another, quiet place where there was less rage and misery. He felt a sense of release and a calmness he'd forgotten existed.

He knew his cheeks were wet with tears, but they were washing his face and mind, not staining them. He became aware of where he was, that the struggling beneath his hand had weakened. The muffled shouting receded but the wriggling continued until it too, ceased. At the end, they were simply flopping as things stopped working. Verity went limp first. Eddie shortly after.

Tom and Sacha stood immobile, silent. Sacha saw something in his expression, something she hadn't seen for a very long time. It looked like peace but couldn't be. He was crying. Not sobbing, just letting tears flow. Part of her noticed the subtle difference between the two and looking beyond the physical process she was witnessing, hoped she saw a man coming to terms with his life.

They stood that way for a while. Each working on different thought processes. looking each other in the eye for a further minute before releasing their grasp on the bags.

Sacha moved over to Tom and checked that none of his tears had fallen astray and onto the floor. It was dry, his clothing had absorbed any evidence. They had discussed what to do next and got on with it. The bags they turned so that the twist was at the throat, where it could be applied by the user.

Eddie's still damp hands were fisted where the bags had bunched, his sweat proof that he had applied them. The rope Tom had used to immobilise Eddie was removed and allowed to fall back into its place on the rig. They spent some time arranging Eddie's hands in a carefully thought-out tangle. Anyone finding this would have no difficulty imagining what had happened. Eddie, the rigger, had bagged his sister and then himself. But something had gone wrong, his hands had gotten snagged. Perhaps he'd panicked or passed out. It didn't matter, the end was result was the same. They'd suffocated during a sex game gone wrong. A tragic accident. All that aside, who'd really care.

Tom moved over to the laptop and studied it. The Twins had used the DVD to watch their trophy. Going through the files on the hard drive he could find no evidence of a backup copy so made one himself and left it as an icon on the desktop entitled 'Fun'. He burned another DVD using a sterile one they'd brought for that purpose. Staining it with The Twins fingerprints, he put the original back in the drive and the hard copy in a sideboard drawer. Mummy had supplied it and if she was first on the scene, was sure to look for it.

The chances of her finding the second copy were small and when the Police visited the crime scene, the disc, or evidence of it, needed to be found. Sacha picked up the phone. Tom turned up the central heating, the house needed to be warm for full effect. Extraction was at 1am.

It was a combination of events that led to the discovery of the bodies twelve days later. Mummy was in the habit of communicating with The Twins at least once a week, usually by phone. When they hadn't picked up or called back and knowing the sort of things they were fond of, as soon as she could get away she had no other option other than to hot foot it down to Devon herself. This was unplanned and an annoyance, she had far too much to do and driving to Devon was not her favourite thing. She'd have to be careful though, to set her face straight when she got there. The Twins resented interference and could be unnerving if challenged.

Someone at the monitoring company eventually noticed that their tags, while switched on and apparently fully operational, were static and had been for some time. That report was shuffled across a desk or two and eventually escalated to Probation. The Twins case officer wasn't a huge fan, she found them creepy and always felt as if she were under some kind of microscope.

Having the option of sending the Police to have a nose around was infinitely preferable to attending herself.

Meantime, their bodies were degrading, the scene deteriorating. Tom had read up on the decay rate of the human body and was surprised and gratified to learn that things can get disgusting quite quickly, particularly in a warm environment.

Rigor Mortis is the tidy part and depending on ambient temperature and other factors, begins shortly after death and can last anything from 24 to 48 hours. The blood settles in the lower part of the body which in the case of The Twins is constricted by rope under pressure from the weight of their corpses, after a few hours, the pooled blood becomes fixed and will never flow again.

At this point, things are still fairly civilised. Loved one's can still be recognised and wept over but once rigor mortis passes, the skin, no longer under muscle control, succumbs to gravity, relaxing into its surroundings, forming new shapes, and accentuating prominent bones.

The next stage, putrefaction, is where things start getting nasty and follows a predetermined timetable, again, dependent upon the warmth of the environment. After 36 hours or so, the neck, abdomen, shoulders, and head begin to turn green.

Bacteria gets busy and that activity produces an accumulation of gas that bloats the body but is most visible around the face where the eyes and tongue protrude as the trapped gas pushes them forward out of the head.

As the putrefaction continues, large amounts of fluid gather, forming blisters. Hair falls out and fingernails begin to sink back into the fingers. As the process remorselessly continues, gathering pace, after eight to ten days, The Twins will be almost black-green, and the fluids will start looking for a way out. As a rule, this is from the mouth and nose, but other orifices are available. Their skin will then start to break open, splitting, releasing gas and fluids into their surroundings, in this case, their living room.

This was the scene the Police strolled into. At the request of the Probation Officer, a car had been sent round to the farmhouse. It was the smell that assailed them first, but reluctant, further investigation revealed the bizarre scene in the living room. Reinforcements and specialists were slow to arrive. The crime scene had barely been ringed by tape when Mummy reached the end of her journey from London.

She had little time for the Police nor them for her, each party regarding the other with a barely concealed contempt.

The senior officer on site was made aware of Mummy's presence by increased noise levels and activity at the head of the gravel driveway. She was demanding access and levelling all manner of legal threats at the young copper who barred her way.

"It's alright Constable. You can let her through."

"And who are you?" She demanded. She had to get into that house, talk to the children before they incriminated themselves. Hide things.

"Detective Inspector Johnson. Devon Police."

"I take it you know who I am?" Her voice was annoying him with its presumption and arrogance. Also, he knew lots of very recent developments that he presumed she didn't but nevertheless, decided that caution should be his watchword.

"I do."

"I want to see my children. You know what will happen if you obstruct me in any way?"

Johnson did. She had a record of forcing sackings, resignations, and early retirements, not only amongst the Police but in the Judiciary and Government.

The woman was a walking, fucking nightmare and Johnson had no intention of preventing her from seeing her children, in fact, he was more than happy to expedite it.

These human rights parasites had no idea of the aftereffects of their crusades. Once their part was over, they'd march off into the sunset to find another righteous cause to pursue while behind them, some low life who should have been put away for a very long time wasn't just out on the street, he had compensation in his pocket. Oh no. Johnson had no intention of obstructing Mrs. Christian.

He stood aside, waving his officers away and following in her wake. He stopped short of the front door. He'd seen all he needed to and much he wished he hadn't. Those two were a mess, hanging there bloated and stinking, dripping onto the rug. He'd wait until she came out before asking about the DVD they'd found.

Epilogue

The Jedi had gone, the parting sudden and unsentimental. They didn't do goodbyes apparently, though they did go so far as to leave them with a private number, with instructions to use it if they ever needed anything. The house seemed empty without them, and Tom and Sacha lacked purpose.

Tom had been uncertain about what might happen next but two days after Devon, she'd sat him down and talked about a future. Their future. If it was ok with him, she'd let their old house out and move in here, with him. From there, they'd take things as they came. The next day, they drove over and cleared her personal stuff out and taking down the canvasses of Ellen, had rehung them here. Tom was easy in their presence. He could look at her now. The immediate future was filled with hours, then days of waiting for The Twins to be found. After that, if they'd left no trace and no fingers were pointed, the world was their oyster.

"We could always buy an old, classic car and drive around the country solving crimes." He'd joked.

Sacha talked about doing some good with the money they had left. There was more than they would ever need and there had to be something they could get involved in, if not at home, then abroad. First though, they talked about a holiday, somewhere in the sun.

What they didn't talk about, was what they'd done. They knew they were satisfied, had a sense that natural justice had reasserted itself and a balance restored and while they'd never be free of events or scars, they were as happy as circumstances allowed, content even, but the nervousness stayed with them, hanging around like a bad smell, they needed to know that they were free and clear before any of their ideas could become a reality. They had no idea how news of The Twins would reach them, only that it would.

Tom and Sacha sat quietly in the kitchen with breakfast, Pooh nestled in a corner of the kitchen, dozing, until disturbed by the muted ringing of a phone. From habit, Tom had kept his old phone charged though it never rang, hadn't for a while, until now. Frowning. Tom retrieved it from a drawer. Unknown caller. Usually, he would have ignored it and let the answerphone do its job, filtering out unwanted intrusions but given recent events and the fact that it was his old phone ringing, his curiosity was piqued so he hit the answer button.

"Mr. Hood?"

"Yes."

"Ah. Good. You may remember me? Inspector Stuart Ames, or at least I was. Retired now."

"Oh. Hello Inspector. It's been a while." Tom's heart thumped. This voice from the past could only have one reason for resurfacing.

"Yes. I'll get straight to the point. There's been an incident, well accident, to be more precise. We wanted to tell you personally. I was asked because this isn't an official contact."

"Contact for what? About what?"

"The Christian Twins."

Tom had rehearsed this next part. This was it. They'd considered that it might be the Police, Press or some other agency but Ames he hadn't thought about for years. He lowered his tone to that of an angry, aggrieved victim.

"An accident? Nothing trivial, I hope."

"Oh no. Quite final. Both dead. I thought you'd like to know."

Tom allowed the proper amount of time before replying, "I suppose I should ask how."

"It'll be in the papers. I'm sending a car over to you now with the latest editions. I thought you'd like to know exactly what happened or at least how it's being reported."

Tom lightened his voice, still role playing. "I appreciate that Inspector. I've moved though, wherever you've sent your car, I'm no longer there."

The gate buzzer sounded. Tom stood and walking to the window, looked down the drive.

"I take it you can see the car, Mr. Hood?"

"How did you know?"

"I know lots of things Mr. Hood. Most of which I'll take to my grave. Please give my regards to Sacha. I truly hope that comes to something. You can safely assume that unless you give anyone reason to interfere further, you won't be hearing from me again."

Anything Tom had rehearsed went straight out of the window. Why would a retired Policeman know where he lived, and that Sacha and he had reunited? Surely their lives weren't that important?

"Safely assume?"

Tom listened to the breathing on the other end of the phone. He got the sense that Ames had more to say, a sense of him knowing more.

"I never forgot your little girl. Mr. Hood. Whether by accident or design, those two got exactly what they deserved. No-one is looking too hard beyond that."

"I'm not sure what to say to that, Inspector."

"I wouldn't say anything, Tom. Certainly not anything that might give anyone cause to believe this was anything other than an accident. Good luck to you both."

The call clicked off. Sacha was looking at him quizzically.

He strolled over to the gate intercom and pressed to open the gate.

"The papers are here."

Ames terminated the call. Perhaps he shouldn't have made it, maybe he should have let sleeping dogs lie but he simply couldn't resist letting Tom and Sacha know that as long as they chose to be, they were free and clear.

He'd timed his onward journey about right, the estate entrance was just a little further and getting in could be complicated if you forgot protocols. Ames was intimate with the estate and its entry systems and while no security set up was unbreachable, this place was as good as it got. Getting out of the car, he placed his thumb on the recognition pad and waited for the massive gates to swing open. In time, they did so, moving easily on huge, stainless-steel wheels and hinges. Driving through them, he waited as they swung closed behind him, locking with a hiss of compressed air as solid steel rams secured them shut. To his front was a second gate, equally imposing and to his left and right, high brick walls. He was in what was essentially, a pen. The enclosure was large enough to accommodate an articulated lorry and covered by an array of cameras, he knew the gate to his front wouldn't open until the main gate behind him was secure and he and his vehicle had been scanned. Aware he was being electronically studied, he sat it out. Someone somewhere was clearly satisfied, and the internal gate opened.

He drove through the grounds, constantly aware of scrutiny, observing motion activated cameras traversing, watching him, silent and unblinking.

Passing the unobtrusive entrance to the old underground nuclear bunker, the extent of which never ceased to surprise him, he drove the remaining hundred yards or so up to the wide frontage of the old Jacobean mansion and pulling up into the parking area, noted that Ollie must be about somewhere, his battered Triumph Spitfire out of place amongst the euroboxes everybody else chose to drive.

The routine today would be different to the norm, so he bypassed his office and took the elevator to the top floor, it stopped, and the doors slid open. Another pen, this one thickly carpeted, the walls a stark white apart from more cameras and a single imposing oak door. He knocked on it. It clicked, indicating that it was now unlocked, and he pushed it open. He'd been here on many occasions but never quite got used to the array of large, high-definition TV screens that were the only wall decorations. Constantly scrolling, they indicated the state of the markets worldwide. A large desk by the window was perfectly positioned to view all of them simultaneously. Other than that, the place was furnished much as a living room would be, leather sofa's occasional tables, lamps and the like. Three doors led to what he knew were a kitchen, a bedroom, and a bathroom. It was where Peter Christian lived and breathed.

Authors Notes

Inevitably, for some stories, the inspiration is taken from life. That is particularly true in the case of 'Swans'. In the early 1990's, an horrific, headline murder took place in the UK. An incomprehensible, evil, apparently random act of cruelty, carried out by children, on a child. Nothing in our culture can prepare a rational human being for such an incident. Nothing.

In 2001, the killers were released. I struggled with the notion that in any crime of this nature, the perpetrators lives get back on track while for the victims, time has a way of standing still. This is where this book began. It was never intended for publication; it was just a personal mechanism for working my way through the supposed penalty for the taking of a life; a way of trying to make sense of a warped legal system and then to satisfy myself that justice had been done. A novel gave me that freedom, my internal proviso, first, do no harm. In that vein, I made every effort to avoid drawing comparisons to any individuals, living or dead.

When the last keystroke was made and I was ready to set it aside, my wife, Julie, took it up, became interested, found errors, corrected them, made suggestions, and gradually became a passionate editor. Over time and through the modern medium of self-publishing, it found its way to you.

There was never any intention for 'Swans' to be anything other than a stand-alone creation. But Tom and Sacha have become part of our lives. We care about them and so it seems, do you.

If you can, please find the time to leave a review on Amazon. Others have and they are now part of the story. It's the little things.

You can find us on Facebook.

We Were Swans

We respond to all comms, and you will also find reviews and additional information relating to this novel. Other books in this series;

Book Two: Tell Me There's a Reason

Book Three: Just a Badge

Now available on Amazon.

Thank You

Printed in Great Britain
by Amazon